Lucie was trembling with sudden anger

"We *will* be together, darling," Julian said placatingly to his wife. "I've already told you I'll be down every weekend."

"You've got it all worked out, haven't you?" Lucie rounded on him. "Is there anything else you've decided without consulting me? Or perhaps you've forgotten that marriage is supposed to be a partnership?"

"Julian, dear," Mrs. Summerford interrupted, "don't lose your temper now. Lucie's overwrought and excited."

"I am not!" Lucie flared. "And I wish you'd mind your own business!"

"How dare you speak to mother like that!" Julian said angrily. "She's only trying to—"

"She's trying to separate us!" Lucie cried. "Can't you see that, or are you blind?" She flung away, ignoring Julian's cry of "Lucie!" as she ran out of the room.

Harlequin Presents Collection

A new series....of old favorites!

Harlequin has been publishing its widely read *Presents* series for more than eight years. These beautiful romance novels, written by the world's most popular authors of romantic fiction, have become the No. 1 best-selling love stories in more than eighty countries.

Now we are pleased to make available to you, our more recent readers, a chance to enjoy many of the early *Presents* favorites you may have missed.

We know you'll enjoy these carefully selected volumes. They come from our not-too-distant past—a past we are proud of, a past we are sure you'll love!

ROBERTA LEIGH

beloved ballerina

Originally published as Harlequin Presents #64

Harlequin Books

TORONTO • LONDON • LOS ANGELES • AMSTERDAM
SYDNEY • HAMBURG • PARIS • STOCKHOLM • ATHENS • TOKYO

Harlequin Presents edition published August 1974
ISBN 0-373-15024-5

Second printing September 1977
Third printing October 1977
Fourth printing March 1979

This *Harlequin Presents Collection* edition published August 1981

Original hardcover edition published in 1953
by The Hutchinson Publishing Group

Printed in U.S.A.

CHAPTER I

"LAST act, beginners on stage, please!"

The call-boy's voice rang through the bare corridors of the theatre and the dressing-room door opened to disgorge a throng of chattering girls, their short skirts bobbing as they made last-minute adjustments to their tights and frilly petticoats. Trooping downstairs, the harsh, uneven lights on the stairway gave their faces an unreal garishness, the eyes unnaturally large and accentuated, the mouth intensely red and the outline of the cheeks vivid with thick paint.

The sounds of the orchestra drifted towards them as they made their way on to the sides of the stage and awaited their cue. Then like white wraiths they floated on, forgetful of their fatigue as they surrendered themselves to the music and formed patterns of movement behind the isolated figures of the solo dancers – swaying, grouping, poising for an instant before they glided poignantly across the stage, their wide skirts delicately luminous. As the dance reached its climax they swirled in a muslin haze, the arms curved, the flowing lines pliant and rhythmic; then the music gradually died away, the curtain fell, and one by one the white figures drifted off into the wings, leaving the principals to acknowledge the applause.

The weary climb back to the dressing-room began and breathless chatter broke out among the girls.

"Don't feel much like this do tonight, do you, Sandra?"

"No, but I'm ravenous, and if we get a good feed it'll be worth going!"

"Well, you can count on that at Mimi's. She loves to think she might be feeding a future Fonteyn! Cheer up, Lucie, it'll soon be over."

This last remark was addressed to a small girl with honey-coloured hair drawn smoothly back above a wide, high brow. Her cheek-bones fell away to a gently curved jaw, their hollows giving her a wistful air accentuated by elongated hazel eyes and a soft, full mouth. She was finely made, with narrow shoulders and hips, and from behind could have been mistaken for a boy. When she spoke her voice was, in keeping with her appearance, light and soft.

"I'm tired, that's all. Madame Molina kept me at the barre for two hours after you left this morning."

"You can blame Piers for that," another girl said. "He's marked you out for something or I'm a Dutchman."

"Not according to Molina," Lucie replied. "She almost called me an elephant today. In the end it degenerated into an endurance test for both of us."

Her muscles aching with fatigue, she pulled herself up the stairs, thinking longly of her quiet bedroom at Ma Cromarty's boarding-house. But Mimi Delfont was a wealthy patroness of the ballet and if any of them did not go to the party she was giving, Madame Molina would want a better excuse than tiredness.

Back in the dressing-room once more they began to unlace their shoes, ripping off their tights and struggling with the hooks of their dresses. Lucie edged to her place at the long, brightly-lit dressing-table with its naked light-bulbs, and began to cream off her make-up, the strident colours merging together in a greasy sheen as she wiped them away on a tissue, revealing the pale transparency of her skin.

Without her stage make-up and in a plain amber-coloured dress a few shades deeper than her hair she looked far more colourless than in the frilly tutu she had just discarded, the brightness of her lipstick only accentuating her pallor. Securing the fine fall of straight hair with two tortoiseshell combs, she joined the stream of girls making their way down to the stage door, and got into one of the taxis Madame Molina had ordered at Mimi Delfont's request.

Their hostess's palatial lounge was already full of people when they arrived, and the hum of conversation mingled with the clinking of glasses and popping of champagne corks. Mimi Delfont greeted them effusively and enjoined them to help themselves at the buffet then, feeling she had done her duty turned her attention back to the principal members of the company, leaving the corps de ballet to fend for themselves.

Disregarding an offer of sandwiches with withered edges and an opportunity of dissecting the evening performance, Lucie surreptitiously edged into a corner and intercepted a waiter with a glass of champagne. She drank it quickly hoping it would lift her tiredness, but it merely made her lightheaded and she looked around for somewhere to sit. Slowly the room began to revolve and she was wondering if she could slip away unnoticed when someone took her arm and propelled her towards a chair.

"Here, take it easy! You're as white as a sheet."

Lucie sank down gratefully and looked up at her rescuer. He was a tall young man of about thirty with straight black hair, a high forehead and thin-cut features. His eyes, although brown, were shadowed by thick, jutting eyebrows which gave him an appearance of fierceness belied by a disarmingly gentle smile.

"I thought you were going to faint at my feet," he said. "Would you like me to get you a drink?"

"I've already had one – that's why you had to come to my rescue. I've been working so hard all day I've hardly had time to eat."

"We'll have to remedy that. What would you like?"

"Anything that's expensive," she said solemnly.

"Foie gras, salmon or caviar, leaving out the sardines, hard-boiled eggs and cheese, I presume?"

She nodded. "Right first time."

He moved away with a laugh and returned a few minutes later with a full plate, watching her as she started to eat.

"Are you at the Dennison School?"

She swallowed a mouthful. "I was, but I'm in the corps de ballet now."

"You look too young to be a fully-fledged dancer."

"Only half-fledged, I'm afraid," she said ruefully. "Still a lot of feathers to grow."

"You've got plenty of time."

"I'm twenty-three."

"A ripe old age!" he grinned.

"Quite ripe for a ballet dancer. Don't forget we start very young." Involuntarily she put up her hand to hide a yawn.

"Little girls should be in bed."

"To tell you the truth I wish I was, but I shall have to leave when all the others do because of the taxis, and that may be hours yet."

"Do you live far from here?"

"Bayswater."

"Well, I shan't be staying very long and I can drop you if you like. It's not much out of my way."

She smiled up at him. "It's very kind of you."

"Not at all. I'll come back for you in a few minutes. There are some people I want to talk to first."

He excused himself and she watched him walk across the room, then closed her eyes and gave herself up to a delicious drowsiness.

"Wake up, lazy-bones!" Another voice broke in on her. "You're not supposed to go to sleep at a party, even if you *are* a wallflower."

Lucie opened her eyes and looked up reproachfully at the young man surveying her. "Lazy-bones be blowed – I've been at the barre nearly all day!"

He grinned wickedly. "Never mind, it's good for you. The old girl's pleased."

She sat up. "Is she really, Piers? Did she say so?"

"She did." The man leaned against the wall, a slight figure with a pointed face and almond eyes set far apart. His winging eyebrows gave him a faun-like appearance accentuated by his habitually quizzical expression, and his every gesture had the lithe fluidity of a dancer. The premier danseur of the Dennison Ballet Company at twenty-nine, Piers Bellamy was beginning to substitute his passionate interest in dancing for the complexities of choreography.

"I'm starting work on a new ballet," he went on. "At the moment Dennison's still arguing, but I think he'll give it a trial. He's willing to let me rehearse the corps de ballet myself, but I shall have to find someone to dance the pas de deux because Adana won't learn it unless she's sure it'll go into the repertoire."

"Do you really think he'll take it?"

"Not unless he's seen it, and even then it depends on his mood. At the moment he refuses to think of me as a choreographer at all and wants me to stick to dancing."

"That's because he doesn't want to lose you," Lucie said staunchly.

He shrugged. "It's just a matter of wearing him down. Come

in early tomorrow morning, Lucie. I'd like to try some of the new routine out with you."

"Me?"

"Yes, you. Don't look so surprised."

"But I didn't think I was good enough!"

"You may not be, yet, but I want to give you a trial." He moved away from the wall. "Come on, you look tired. I'll take you home."

"It's awfully nice of you, Piers, but I've already been offered a lift." She gestured towards the opposite corner of the room. "The man over there – I don't know his name."

"A dancer?"

"I shouldn't think so."

Piers lost interest. "In that case I'll be getting along. Don't forget to come in early tomorrow."

Almost as soon as he had gone the dark young man reappeared.

"Managed to keep awake?" His brown eyes glinted with amusement. "I half expected to find you asleep on your nose."

"Not quite," she smiled. "Are you ready now?"

"Yes, let's go."

They said goodnight to their hostess and made their way through the wide hall and down the steps to one of the cars standing by the kerb.

"Infernal nuisance, these parties." He let in the clutch and they moved off.

"Why do you go if you don't like them?"

"Matter of having to. Mrs. Delfont's a friend of my mother's and I have to put in an occasional appearance to prove I don't spend all my leisure running from night club to night club."

"You don't look the type for that," she said, "even if you did pick me up!"

"You'd have fallen down otherwise!"

"Don't remind me – I felt awful."

They chattered desultorily about the party and the ballet, and as they drew up at the front door of the boarding-house Lucie held out her hand.

"Thanks for the lift, Mr. –?"

"Summerford," he said. "Which reminds me, I don't know *your* name."

"Lucinda Marlow."

"What an imposing name for a slip of a thing like you! Sleep well, sprite."

He waited until she had climbed the steps before he called a final good night and Lucie watched the tail-light of his car disappear and wondered if she would ever see him again.

She was at the theatre early the following morning to find Piers already limbering up at the barre, and three hours passed before they left the practice-room. This was the first of many tedious rehearsals and for the next few weeks she spent the mornings learning the dance he had devised. It was the first time she had ever broken away from the corps de ballet and not even the thought that Dennison might not accept the new choreography could quell her enthusiasm. Piers was an arduous task-master who complained bitterly if she flagged, but he drove himself just as hard and gradually the dance took shape, absorbing so much of their energy that it made their nightly performance and the daily practice with the rest of the company seem unimportant by comparison.

Lucie was completely familiar with the routine by the time Piers asked Jack Dennison to see it. She was as apprehensive as a novice when he finally appeared in the practice-room one morning and eased his great bulk into one of the creaky wicker chairs, his leonine head reflected scores of times in the mirrors lining the walls. But she gained confidence from Piers who studiously ignored their audience and threw himself into the dance he had created, a pas de deux set to a Scarlatti sonata which the indifferent pianist hammered from the ancient piano.

Dennison's head nodded several times as it came to an end. "Good, good." The deep voice held genuine satisfaction. "One day you will do well as a choreographer, Piers." The tired eyes shifted to the girl. "And you, my dear – in three, perhaps even two years, you may be ready to tackle big parts."

Lucie sat down on the floor, looking like a boy in her black tights, and Piers wiped his forehead. "Lucie's not warm enough for the part yet, Jack. She needs more abandonment. But she's given you an idea of how the dance will look and that's the main thing. Will you take it?"

The heavy shoulders moved expressively. "It is good, but

too insubstantial. It lacks depth. A little longer, perhaps . . ."

"That's only the final pas de deux," Piers said shortly. "When I've worked out the rest of it, it'll be quite long enough."

"Well, show it to me again when it is finished. Then I will consider it."

Piers made a gesture of irritation. "But I don't want to go on working on it if you won't take it."

"You are too impatient, Piers. One can never be sure of one's market before the goods are made. Let me see it again when it's ready."

With a grunt Dennison heaved himself up and Piers regarded the retreating figure ironically.

"Well, Lucie, more work ahead." He pulled her to her feet. "Let's go and have some coffee. I must put my thinking cap on."

"Dennison talks so glibly about two or three years," she said, as they walked out of the room. "I don't suppose it seems long to him, but it's a lifetime to me."

He grinned. "Now who's being impatient? But he's not always right, you know. I don't think it'll take you as long as that. You need to let yourself go a bit more, but you're good already."

Her face lit up. "Do you really think so?"

"I do. Determination is half the battle, and you seem to have plenty of that."

"I need it. Heaven knows I get discouraged easily enough."

"Well, don't. You'll never get to the top if you are."

But Lucie's disappointment was more for Piers than herself. Although well aware that if the ballet was accepted she would not be given a chance to dance it with him, she did not begrudge having to spend every free hour in the practice-room. Gradually the choreography took shape and when Piers began to concentrate on the other parts Lucie reverted to normal routine. She was shaken out of it again when Madame Molina told her that Dennison had decided to give her the part of The Blue Bird in their new production of The Sleeping Beauty, and did not know whether to be delighted or afraid. Although well within her range, it was a severe test of characterisation, and her hardest task was to master the variations without losing the appropriate expression. But although she felt herself inadequate, Dennison seemed satisfied, and his brief words of approval meant a great deal to her.

The first night of The Sleeping Beauty found the company in its usual state of nervous exhaustion and everything seemed to go wrong. Shoes would not stay on, buttons and shoulder-straps burst, tights wrinkled and head-dresses slipped. But once the curtain went up everything was perfect and the stimulus of the orchestra reached out and enveloped the anxious dancers.

As the time for her entrance drew near Lucie stood trembling in the wings with her partner, a young man who was also making his first solo appearance and was equally nervous. But at last a soft refrain gave them their cue and they stepped out on to the stage to begin their pas de deux.

In the third row of the stalls Julian Summerford studied his programme, surprised to see that the quiveringly alive figure in blue was the shy, nondescript girl he had met at Mimi Delfont's party. Off-stage her personality had been completely negative, but seeing her under the lights, swaying and twisting in her partner's arms, she seemed to embody the very spirit of the dance, and had a subtle beauty and elegance of line that made her lovely to watch. At the end of the pas de deux he joined in the enthusiastic applause and decided to go round to the stage door after the performance to congratulate her and ask her out to supper.

Lucie flushed with pleasure when she read his note, surprised that he had remembered her after all. As always after a first night everyone was in high spirits, and she was eager for gaiety and praise. For once she did not feel like talking "shop" with the other girls and it was pleasant to think she would not have to return to a warmed-up supper and a cup of cocoa in her lodgings.

Julian Summerford regarded her curiously when she ran down to meet him at the stage door, faintly disappointed that she looked exactly the same as when he had seen her at the party – a little more colourless, in fact, compared with the vital figure she had been on the stage.

"I hope I haven't kept you waiting?" she asked politely.

He smiled at her ingenuousness. "You've been very quick,

considering the transformation. Thank you for accepting my invitation. What would you like to do?"

"Eat," she said promptly, and preceded him into the street.

He opened the car door for her. "You're the first woman I've met who isn't ashamed to say she's hungry!"

"Then you can't have known many dancers – we're always hungry! Incidentally, thanks for the compliment."

"What compliment?"

"Calling me a woman. Last time we met I was only a little girl!"

"When you say that you sound more than ever like a little girl. But I won't tease you too much after your lovely Blue Bird."

"Oh, did you like it?" she asked eagerly. "I'm afraid my arabesques weren't up to much."

"Don't talk technicalities to me – I'm a ballet fan, not an expert."

"But you know what an arabesque is, don't you?" she asked wonderingly.

"Yes, but I've no intention of letting you talk shop – at least not until you've had something to eat. Shall we go to Rules?"

"I've never been there."

"I'm surprised. It's a well-known theatrical haunt."

"I don't go out much," she admitted candidly. "Usually too busy working."

He glanced at her but said nothing, and a few minutes later they drew up outside the little restaurant.

Lucie was delighted with the little restaurant whose walls were covered with photographs of old music-hall artists and playbills of generations past and gone; in this atmosphere she felt at home and was completely at ease with Julian. She thought him even more striking-looking than she had remembered, his dark, thin face and nervous hands completely at variance with his gentle manner and unobtrusive personality. He was totally unlike the decisive young men in the ballet, his calm ambition quite different from their passionate determination to succeed.

She ate a stalwart meal and Julian enjoyed her obvious appreciation of the food, amused that so small a person could eat so much. Although his first sight of Lucie had almost made him regret his invitation, he changed his mind as the evening progressed, for she took on the warmth and colour of her surroundings, and the evening passed so quickly that it was closing time before he realised they were the last diners in the room. He apologised as he moved the table out for her.

"I should have realised you'd be tired after your first night and taken you home earlier."

"I am a bit sleepy," she admitted, "but it's been such fun I wouldn't have cut it short for anything. The only snag is that I've got to be at the theatre early."

"More rehearsals?" He helped her on with her coat.

"A work-out with Piers Bellamy. He's doing the choreography of a new ballet and I'm learning the principal part so he'll have some idea how it'll look with Adana."

"Pretty thankless task, isn't it?"

"Oh, no," she said quickly. "I'm lucky to have been chosen."

"All that work for nothing, though – it'll wear you out." He held the door open for her and she pirouetted out into the street, the full skirt of her coat billowing around her.

"Ballet dancers should be like racehorses and greyhounds, thin and sinewy!" She held out a slender leg. "Feel how strong the muscles are."

Amused at her naïve pride he bent and gripped her calf, the steely muscles tensing as he enclosed them. She swayed and almost fell before he steadied her.

"You may be as sinewy as a greyhound, but you're not a stork by any stretch of the imagination!"

Laughing, they got into the car and a few moments later were driving through the ghostly emptiness of Covent Garden. Lucie shivered and he bent forward and switched on the heater.

"Better?"

"Much better, thanks." She looked around her. "This is an awfully nice car. What is it?"

"A Bentley."

She was suitably impressed. "What do you do for a living?"

He smiled slightly. "I'm in the Foreign Office."

"Oh, a diplomat – I shall have to mind my p's and q's! What's your first name? You only signed your note J. Summerford."

"Give you three guesses."

"John, Joseph or James," she said promptly.

"Wrong. It's Julian."

"What a nice name! You look like a Julian."

"And what's your idea of a Julian?"

"Someone tall, dark and handsome – with a Bentley."

He laughed. "I'm glad I fill the bill. What about you? All I know is your name, and I'm not even sure whether that's your real one."

"Oh, yes, I haven't got a stage name. My friends call me Lucie."

"What made you want to be a dancer?"

"My mother was one until she married. Daddy was a country G.P., but I followed in her footsteps and went to the Dennison school when I was ten. We danced all the morning and had ordinary lessons in the afternoon."

"They won't take you above a certain age, will they?"

"No, you've got to start while your limbs are still malleable."

He grimaced. "It sounds like some form of torture! I can't imagine anyone wanting to take it up! I don't suppose you have much time for outside interests, do you?"

She smiled. "The ballet is my only interest. I can't imagine my life without it. You're right about it being exacting, though. If you want to be a ballet dancer you've got to give up practically everything else. And even if you get to the top you have to go on working just as hard. You've got to want to be a dancer more than anything else in the world, otherwise you'd never stick it."

"You've stuck it pretty well up to now. Personally I'd have chosen something a bit easier."

"Dancing is the only thing that satisfies me."

He rounded a bend and changed gears. "Well, your parents must be very proud of you."

"Daddy died when I was fifteen," she said quietly, "and my mother died two years ago."

"I'm sorry."

As he spoke they drew up outside the boarding-house and she held out her hand. "Thank you for a lovely evening, I enjoyed it very much."

"I enjoyed it too," he smiled.

She had her key in the lock before she was aware that he had followed her up the steps. "When can I see you again?"

"Whenever you like," she said simply.

"Good. Then I'll call for you at the theatre one night later this week. Good night, Lucie."

"Good night – Julian."

CHAPTER II

For the next few months Julian called for Lucie at the theatre two or three times a week and took her out to dinner. He was intrigued by the disparity between her appearance on-stage and off, and charmed by her fresh candour – so different to the sophisticated outlook of the women he was used to. At first he had thought her naïveté a pose, but as he got to know her better he realised that not only was she incapable of pretence but that beneath her gaiety lay intelligence and strength of character.

Lucie loved the evenings she spent with Julian, for he was quite unlike any of the men with whom she normally associated. The ballet was another world to him, not a world in itself as it was to her, and she was continually surprised that he did not know more about something that was as much a part of her life as breathing. But she found his ignorance appealing and his easy good manners and courtly deference were a refreshing change from the easy camaraderie of her fellow dancers.

Almost without Lucie being aware of it, Julian became part of her life. The evenings when they did not meet seemed interminable and not even immersing herself in the performance could take him off her mind. But it was not until he caught influenza and was unable to see her for a week that she realised how much he had come to mean to her, and spent the evenings of his absence veering between rapture and desolation.

It was the first time she had ever been in love and the emotion was so wonderful that she hugged it to herself like a miser. But her desire for secrecy did not last, and she soon longed for Julian to share it and reciprocate her love. From then on her hours with him were bitter-sweet, and she alternated between being hurt at his obtuseness and fear that he might never regard her as anything other than an amusing and slightly odd companion.

They had known each other nearly three months when he rang her up one morning and asked her to dine with him at the Savoy. They usually ate at less pretentious places and Lucie was intrigued at the sudden change of rendezvous.

"Have you come into a fortune?" she asked gaily.

He laughed, the sound coming explosively through the receiver. "I resent that! Has my choice of restaurants always been so humble?"

"You know I always enjoy myself with you," she protested.

"I'm only teasing." There was a moment's pause. "I must go now, the buzzer's ringing. Pick you up after the performance."

Although Julian had denied any special significance in their dining at the Savoy, Lucie sensed a suppressed excitement in him when he called for her at the theatre, and when he suddenly put down his knife and fork at dinner she knew he was going to tell her something important.

"I've been given a new job, Lucie – that's why I brought you here to celebrate."

"So I was right after all! Oh, Julian, I'm so pleased for you – is it a promotion?"

"Not exactly, but it may lead to one."

"What is it?"

"I'm going to act as a liaison at the Three-Power Conference in Paris."

"Paris! Does that mean you'll be going away?"

He avoided her eyes. "Not for long – only about three months."

Only three months – how short a time he made it sound! But the days stretched ahead of her in a vista of loneliness.

"I'll miss you," she said quietly.

"I'll miss you too, but the time will soon pass."

"I'm sure it will."

They were speaking like strangers, stilted and awkward, and Lucie tried desperately to keep the conversation on a normal level.

"Are you looking forward to going?"

"I suppose I am, in a way. Paris is lovely. Do you know it?"

"No, when the company went five years ago I was too young and they haven't been since."

"I was forgetting the ballet's been your whole life." He twirled the stem of his glass. "I wonder if you'd ever be happy away from it?"

Her heart began to thud. "That would depend on why I gave it up."

"If you got married, for instance, and it was impossible for you to go on."

"In that case I'd have to love the man very much."

"But you *would* love a man very much if you married him, wouldn't you, Lucie?"

"Yes."

She lowered her eyes hoping he might say something more, but he glanced instead at his watch.

"Damn, I didn't realise it was so late! I've got an early train to catch tomorrow."

Her eyes lifted quickly. "Are you going so soon?"

"Not to Paris – that's not for a fortnight – but I'm going to Devon to see my family first."

"Then we must leave – you mustn't be late. You really needn't have bothered to take me out at all."

She was sorry the moment the words were said, for he reddened.

"You're tired, Lucie. It's just as well we're going."

She left her coffee unfinished and followed him out to the car, sitting miserably in the corner as they drove off. They were silent for most of the drive, Julian staring intently ahead and Lucie twisting her hands in her lap and wondering what he would say if she suddenly begged him to take her to Paris.

They were nearly at the boarding-house when he reached out and patted her hand. "Poor sweet, don't be upset. It's only three months."

Her voice trembled. "I'm sorry I was rude."

"Forget it."

"But on our last evening..."

"Never mind, you look adorable in a temper!"

He drew up outside the grey stone house and switched off the engine. The night was dark and a street lamp threw shadows across Lucie's face, making her look so young and forlorn that he touched her cheek.

"Don't be miserable, sprite. I won't be away for ever and when I come back I'll get in touch with you immediately."

"Will you really?"

"Of course. I'm very fond of the ballet."

"Only the ballet?"

"And a little dancer called Lucinda Marlow."

She closed her eyes and two tears trickled down her cheeks. "I'm going to miss you too. I love Bentleys."

"Only Bentleys?"

"And the tall, dark, handsome men who drive them."

"Lucie, Lucie!" His arms went round her and he sought her mouth with his. It was the first time they had kissed and he was surprised at the intensity of her response and the sudden tenderness he felt for her. Her lips moved beneath his, warm and yielding, until he put her gently away and smoothed the hair from her forehead. "Good night, little Lucie. Don't forget me."

"I won't," she whispered, and without another word stepped blindly out of the car and ran into the house.

Julian decided to drive down to Devon the following morning rather than go by train. The memory of Lucie's tears lingered disturbingly in his mind and he was glad to leave London behind him. The fields were still shrouded in a fine blanket of snow, but the sun was beginning to melt it when he drove through Dawlish and out along the coast road to Shalford, a small fishing village on a promontory three miles beyond the town of Teincombe. Leaving the village behind, he drove up the narrow lane that curved to the brow of the hill, and at the top turned in between a pair of wrought-iron gates, switched off the engine and glided silently down the sloping drive, coming to a halt at the tall, white door.

The house was quiet and realising everyone was at lunch, he walked through the wide hall into a room at the other side of the house overlooking the garden.

A tall, middle-aged woman with a plump, serene face and smooth dark hair gave an exclamation of pleasure as he came in.

"Julian dear, how lovely to see you! I didn't expect you till this evening."

"Managed to get away early." He kissed her. "Not very keen on long drives after dark."

She returned his kiss warmly. "Have you had lunch?"

"No, I'd love some. I'll just go up and wash my hands."

Walking up the shallow stairs that curved to meet the long

corridor from which all the main bedrooms branched, he thought how good it was to be home. The warmth of the house seemed to envelop him; here he could forget his problems, forget he had a difficult job ahead of him and become once more a cherished son.

His room had already been prepared, even to a bowl of Christmas roses on the dark oak dressing-table, and as he washed he remarked the tablet of pine-scented soap. How like his mother to remember it was his favourite! Humming softly, he shut the door behind him and went down to the dining-room again.

His mother had left the remainder of her meal uneaten and would not continue until he had finished his grapefuit.

"I see so little of you that I don't like eating alone when I don't have to. This room's too large for one person at the best of times."

He threw her an affectionate glance. "You should eat in the breakfast-room when you're alone. By the way, how's Francis?"

"Very well, dear. At least, I think he is. He doesn't tell me very much these days."

"Something to do with Ann again, I suppose?"

"I'm afraid so. The dear girl keeps wanting him to move to London."

"That's ridiculous. His home's here."

"I know, but Ann doesn't think so. She says this house will be yours one day and Francis shouldn't devote himself to the estate. She's making him miserable with her nagging, but I don't want to interfere."

"I quite agree. Their marriage is their own affair and I don't see why you should worry yourself about it. I've a good mind to have a word with Francis. He's got no right to let Ann upset you. Where are they, by the way? I've been looking forward to seeing the twins. Have they had an early lunch?"

Mrs. Summerford smoothed her napkin. "I was going to tell you when you'd finished."

"Tell me what?"

"That Ann and Francis aren't living here any more. They've moved."

"Moved? What on earth for? Where to?"

"Not very far away, dear – about two miles the other side of Shalford. You know Ann's always wanted a home of her own –

although I've done my best to make her feel *this* is her home – and she's finally persuaded Francis to buy a little house. Of course it's nothing like this – they've no separate nursery for the children, for instance – but Ann was so set on it that I don't think Francis could hold out against her any longer, although he did put his foot down about going to London. He still helps Mr. Hardy with the estate, so I suppose we have that much to be thankful for."

Julian gestured impatiently. "I simply don't understand Ann wanting to move into a poky little house when she could have stayed on here with you."

"Ah well, young women like to be independent these days." Mrs. Summerford served the meat. "I even offered to have the top floor made into a flat for them, but she wouldn't hear of it. Her excuse was that you might marry one day and want to bring your wife here, although I told her you've got your career to think of and wouldn't dream of tying yourself down yet. But nothing I said could make her change her mind and I had to accept her decision whether I liked it or not. It isn't very far away, so I still see Francis every day – he finds it more convenient to have lunch here rather than go back to Mayfields. But today is Ann's birthday, so of course he felt he had to have lunch with her."

"Her birthday – so it is! And I forgot to get her a present."

"Never mind. I sent her a pair of silver candlesticks from us both – the little ones on my dressing-table she's always liked so much."

Julian laid his hand over hers. "You're too good, Mother. We none of us deserve it – least of all Ann."

"Nonsense. What use am I if I can't be good to my children?"

"Don't talk like that – you're the pivot of all our lives."

She smiled tremulously. "Just to hear you say that makes everything worth-while. Sometimes I feel like giving up the house altogether and following you wherever you're sent. You need me to make a home for you – I hate to think of you living at some stuffy club or hotel. But then I'm frightened of being a burden on you, so I stay here and wait for you to come back to me."

"As if you could ever be a burden, Mother! Surely you know

how much it means to me to come home and find everything the same?"

"I'm glad. I want everything to be the same always."

But somehow the graciousness of his home did not bring Julian the usual satisfaction, and not even visiting Francis and Ann at their unpretentious new home and playing with his twin nephews could rid him of a vague disquiet. One afternoon as they were having tea in the drawing-room his mother remarked on his restlessness.

"What's the matter, Julian – don't you feel well?"

He walked to the wide sweep of windows and looked down across the sloping lawns to the sea, which was almost as grey as the sky. "Perhaps I'm just tired, Mother. It seems harder to settle down here this time after the last few months in town."

"They work you too hard, darling. I shall write to Maggie Ranken and tell her Sir John should give you more time off."

Julian laughed and turned to survey the figure sitting so upright over the tea trolley, legs decorously crossed at the ankles, violet skirts falling in graceful folds around her.

"I'm not a schoolboy any longer, Mother. Sir John would never let me forget it if his wife said anything to him about overworking me."

"Silly boy, I knew John when he was younger than you are now! I almost married him, but your father came along and swept me off my feet." She sighed. "How sad that he didn't live to see you and Francis grow up. Do you ever think of him?"

His mother so rarely spoke of his father that Julian sensed her disquiet.

"You're not brooding, are you, Mother?"

"Brooding?"

"About Francis and Ann."

Mrs. Summerford studied her wedding-ring thoughtfully. "I suppose I must have been thinking about them quite a lot," she said at last. "It's made me realise that one's children are independent and thoughtless of the sacrifices one has made for them. Sometimes I think it might have been easier if I'd had a daughter. I don't think a girl alters even when she's married, but a man . . ." She shrugged. "A man doesn't want his mother when he has a wife."

Julian sat down on the sofa. "You're not talking sense, darling. Francis loves you as much as ever, but it can make life damned uncomfortable for him if he and Ann are at loggerheads all the time. It's a pity he's had to move, but you see him nearly as much as if he was still living here."

"I suppose you're right, but Ann doesn't like me and I'm afraid she may turn Francis against me too."

"No one can turn your own son against you, and I'm sure Ann has no intention of trying."

"I hope not. Oh, Julian, just to be able to talk to you and unburden all my silly fancies makes me feel so much better! How long will you be here?"

"About a week," he said vaguely. "I'm not sure yet."

He stood up and walked slowly round the room, straightening a picture on the wall and running a hand idly over the keys of the baby grand by the window. The decoration was muted and soft, each object blending with the next, and he was unaccountably reminded of Lucie. What a lovely setting this house would make for her and how she would love it! He could imagine her dancing across to him, her colourless hair flowing back from her face, her large, wide-apart eyes full of pleasure and excitement. Convinced that she existed on cups of tea and stale buns, he thought how good the country air and food would be for her and felt a sudden longing to cherish her.

With a suddenness that took him by surprise he realised it would be unbearable if Lucie ever disappeared. Never to see the laughing face or hold the supple little body in his arms would rob him of something irreplaceable, and in the same instant he knew he could not leave England without seeing her again.

Once he had made up his mind, he pretended he had been recalled to London sooner than he had expected, justifying the lie by telling himself that it was as much in his mother's interest as his own. How could he express his feeling for Lucie when he scarcely knew what it was himself?

Driving back to London four days later his anticipation increased with every mile. He was astonished that such an innocent friendship could have aroused so much emotion in him, and for the first time realised he had only kissed her once since he had known her – had never felt anything but the most fleeting touch of her lips.

He bathed and changed leisurely at his club, knowing Lucie would not be free until late evening, and three hours later parked his car in the narrow alley outside the stage door. At last the girls began to stream out and he peered anxiously through the window, afraid of missing her. But the crowd dwindled and there was still no sign of her and he got out of the car and approached the stage door. Almost at once he heard her voice and the deeper tones of a man echoing down the corridor, and drew back a little to wait until they appeared.

Lucie was wearing the same full-skirted coat she had worn on the evening of their first dinner at Rule's, and her soft hair fell loosely over her shoulders. She was talking to Piers, her face alight with gaiety, and the man drew his arm casually through hers as they came out into the alley.

"Don't go home yet," Piers said. "I want to explain those new steps before we try them out tomorrow. We can have a bite to eat somewhere while we talk."

"That's a good idea." Then: "Darn it, I've forgotten my notebook! Hang on a minute, I'll pop up and get it."

Turning back, she noticed the man standing in the shadows and all movement was arrested, all gaiety wiped from her face.

"Julian!"

With a murmur she flew into his arms and he held her close, feeling her tremble against him.

Lucie drew back first. "I never expected four months to pass so quickly!" She turned to Piers, who was watching with ill-concealed annoyance. "Julian's going to Paris and I thought he'd left already."

"Oh?" Piers regarded Julian sardonically. "What's held you up?"

"Business." He looked at Lucie. "Are you free tonight?"

She hesitated, and Piers nodded ungraciously. "By all means go. But don't forget I want you in the morning."

"I'll be in the practice-room at nine," she promised eagerly.

With a nod the slight figure moved away down the road and Lucie looked guiltily at Julian. "Poor Piers, he wanted to tell me about the new routine."

"Are you disappointed he can't?"

"Of course not – I'm going to be with you." She linked her arm in his. "Are you jealous?"

"Have I reason to be?"

"No. Piers is just part of my work." She shivered. "Come along, it's cold."

He started the engine and the car moved forward.

"Where are we going, Julian?"

"I thought I'd take you dancing for a change."

"That's a busman's holiday with a vengeance! Although it *will* be a change to dance with you."

"I'm afraid I'm not as good as your friend Piers."

"He's hopeless on a dance floor." She giggled softly. "An entrechat or a jeté battû, yes, but definitely not a quickstep!"

"Then you won't be able to compare us."

"I never do." She glanced at him seriously. "It's the first time you've ever spoken like this. What's the matter with you, Julian?"

"I don't know," he confessed. "Probably didn't like seeing you with Bellamy when I'd been looking forward to our meeting. His being there nearly spoilt it."

"But I wasn't expecting you – I didn't think I'd be seeing you again for months."

"Perhaps you're sorry I came?"

Her lips trembled. "If you're trying to hurt me you're succeeding very well."

He put out a hand to squeeze the one lying on her lap. "Forgive me, sprite. Let's forget it."

A few minutes later they drew up at the imposing entrance to a Chelsea restaurant.

"Come along, I've got a table near the floor," he said.

But he would not dance with her until she had eaten the better part of her meal, and plied her with food with a persistent solicitude that she found touching. As she sipped the wine he had ordered a faint colour flushed her skin, and when at last he was satisfied she had eaten enough he stood up and led her on to the dance floor.

Suddenly this moment before he took her into his arms held a thrill of exquisite anticipation and as she moved close a tremor ran through him. She was as wonderful to dance with as he had expected, and looking down at the curve of her eyebrows and sweep of fair lashes he did not know how he could bear to put so many miles between them.

Lucie tried to dismiss the thought that this evening was only an interlude for Julian, but she was miserably aware that it might be the last time she would ever see him and her gaiety was so forced that he noticed it.

"You seem excited tonight, Lucie. What's been happening while I've been away – have you been promoted to ballerina?"

"Good heavens, no! There are years of work ahead of me yet."

"Well, what is it then?"

"It could be that I'm excited at being with you again."

"I hope so," he smiled, "because I came back earlier especially to see you."

"It won't be so easy to see me when you're in Paris."

"I know." He stood up. "Come on, there's our favourite tune. Let's dance."

Sensing his desire to change the subject Lucie followed him on to the floor, willing herself to derive some consolation from the fact that he had cut short his stay in Devon in order to see her before he went.

That night he did not drive her straight home when they left the restaurant but drew up in Hyde Park, bringing the car to a halt beneath a group of trees overlooking the lake. The leaves rustled above them in the darkness and the occasional lights of a passing car threw shadows over the water as Julian took one of her hands and held it to his lips.

"You have lovely hands, sprite. I've never seen such small ones."

"They're strong and capable, Julian."

"I'm sure they are. Lucie, are you really glad I came to see you before I went away?"

"One is always pleased to see old friends," she said sedately.

"Darling, don't tease me!"

"What would you like me to do?"

He drew her against him. "I'd like you to kiss me."

Willingly she gave herself into his arms, her whole being responsive to the gentle urgency of his embrace. They clung together for a long while, then he pushed her tenderly away and twined his fingers in hers.

"Oh, Julian, this week has seemed like a year!" Her voice was muffled against his shoulder. "I've missed you so much."

"And I've missed you, my love." He held her hands against his lips and placed a kiss in each palm. "Look after your hands, my darling, they hold my heart."

During the next few days they saw each other every possible moment. He called for her in the morning and drove her to the theatre; picked her up again for lunch and took her back in time for the performance, leaving her at the stage door to go to his seat in the stalls. To please him she skipped several rehearsals and did not tell him of Piers' anger nor how the dancer ridiculed her excuses. The time passed so quickly that almost before she knew it, it was Julian's last day, and he persuaded her to miss rehearsal for the last time, arranging to call for her at the boarding-house in the morning.

By ten-thirty she was ready at the door, eager not to waste a moment of the time Jack Dennison had grudgingly allowed her, and as the dark green Bentley turned into the street she flew down the steps.

Julian leant forward and opened the door. "Good morning, darling. You were very quick!"

"I've been waiting for you," she said artlessly, and got into the car. "Where are we going?"

"To a hotel I know near the river. I thought you might like to have lunch there, it's rather nice."

They avoided the main morning traffic and reached the hotel just after mid-day. It was too cold to sit on the terrace, and they wandered hand-in-hand across the lawns, only turning back when Lucie said she was hungry.

The dining-room was practically empty and they chose a table in the far corner. It was deliciously warm and Lucie slipped off her coat to reveal a dark blue silk dress, the severity of its cut softened by a collar of coffee-coloured lace almost the same shade as her hair.

"I bought this dress in your honour. Do you like it?"

"Very much, but isn't it rather thin for the winter?"

Her face fell. "I suppose it is, but I couldn't resist it."

"It's lovely anyway, darling," he said consolingly. "You should wear blue more often."

She brightened. "I know; it makes me look less insignificant."

"You're not in the least insignificant."

"Oh, Julian, what a lovely lie! Of course I am, that's part of my charm – at least, I hope so! You can notice me when you want to and ignore me when you don't."

He threw back his head and laughed. "You've far too much personality to be ignored! Nobody overlooks a precocious child, and that's what you remind me of – in the nicest possible way, of course."

"I'm not a child, Julian."

At the sudden change in her expression he set down his fork. "I know you aren't, Lucie, I was only teasing."

She was silent until the waiter had removed their plates. "I don't think you *were* teasing, Julian. You've always thought of me as a child. Would you think of me as a woman if I weren't so small?"

He grinned. "Whatever you do don't get fat, or I won't love you."

"Do you anyway?"

"Do I what?"

"Love me, Julian?"

He took her hand and her heart lurched. "More than anything in the world, Lucie. Will you marry me?"

She flinched. "Don't joke, darling, I can't bear it."

"I'm not joking, Lucie. I was never more serious in my life. Will you marry me?"

"But I –"

"I've got a special licence — had it in my pocket for the last three days, only somehow I couldn't get around to asking you. We can be married at Caxton Hall this afternoon. I'll pull a few strings at the Foreign Office to get your passport through, and you can come with me to Paris."

Her eyes glowed. "Oh, Julian, wouldn't it be wonderful! A runaway marriage, almost like an elopement! I've always wanted to be swept off my feet." Then her face fell. "But what about the ballet – and Piers?"

"Damn the ballet and Piers! You can't sacrifice your whole life to dancing."

"But it *is* my life."

"Well, it won't be any more. *I'm* going to be your life from now on, Lucie. Darling sprite, will you marry me?"

For a moment she looked at him gravely, then the conflict

died out of her face and it was transfigured with love. "Oh yes, Julian. Yes, please."

He stood up quickly. "Let's get out of here! I can't look at you without wanting to kiss you and I don't think the head waiter would like it if I did."

He paid the bill and led her out to the car, kissing her quickly and passionately before he started the engine. "Darling Lucie, you'll never regret it! I swear I'll make you happy."

They were half-way to London when Lucie suddenly remembered Mrs. Summerford.

"Have you told your mother about us?" she asked.

"Not yet, but there'll be plenty of time for her to get used to the idea while we're in Paris."

She laughed. "Surely *we're* the ones who'll have to get used to the idea!"

"That's one way of looking at it, my love, but I don't expect many mothers would see it like that." He drew the car in to the side of the road and turned to face her. "If I'd known I was going to get married when I went down to Devon I'd have told Mother there and then. She's been upset lately about my brother and his wife. Ann's a nice girl, but she's not much of a daughter-in-law and Mother's been rather unhappy about it."

Lucie looked sympathetic. "It's a great pity when a girl doesn't get on with her mother-in-law – it usually makes the husband unhappy too."

"I knew you'd understand, darling." He was relieved. "I'm sure you and Mother will get on famously together."

"I hope so, Julian. We shall have a great bond in loving you."

He bent to kiss her and she threw her arms around his neck and pulled his head down. "Oh, Julian, I'm so happy! When I said good-bye to you that time I thought I'd die."

"My precious darling, what a thoughtless fool I've been!" He nuzzled her cheek. "Will you mind giving up the ballet very much?"

"Perhaps at first, but I'll have you to make up for it. I'd rather have a nice old Mr. Summerford in fifty years' time than be a cranky old ballet mistress, which is what usually happens to us."

"I don't think it would to you, my little ballerina." He tweaked her ear.

"I'm not so sure." Her expression was serious. "Before I met you my career was so important that I couldn't imagine the future without it. Now it all seems rather pointless, and when you're not there to watch me dance the whole theatre's empty."

"I'm glad you feel that way," he said softly, "because you'll have to make me your only audience from now on. You won't be able to go back to the ballet, you know – I shall probably be posted abroad and I don't intend to leave you behind."

She covered his face with kisses. "I wouldn't let you go without me – you're far too attractive to travel on your own!"

He pulled her against him. "You needn't be jealous, my love – I shall never want anyone but you."

Their wedding later that afternoon was not like either of them had imagined, for Lucie had never pictured herself as a bride and if Julian had dwelt on the subject at all it had been to visualise himself waiting for some satined figure walking towards him up the aisle of a church. But he was too absorbed in the girl at his side to notice the austerity of their surroundings, too happy to worry about what his mother would say and convinced that in Lucie she would find the daughter-in-law she had always wanted. What a pity she was not here for the wedding – damn Ann for upsetting her! If it had not been for that, he could have told her about Lucie without feeling he was confronting her with a threatened repetition of the unhappiness Francis's marriage had caused. As things were it would be better to write and explain from Paris.

With a start he realised that the registrar was showing him where to sign and after a few brief formalities the man shook hands with them and wished them good luck.

Walking to the car, Lucie twisted the wedding-ring on her finger and looked down at it admiringly. "This is the first jewellery I've ever worn."

"Thank the Lord for that! I'd hate you to deck yourself out with artificial gew-gaws."

She grimaced. "How awful to dance and jingle at the same time!" Hugging his arm, she went down the steps, then broke away and spun round excitedly. "Mrs. Julian Summerford! –

how nice it sounds! You must treat me with more respect now I'm a married woman."

He bowed low as he opened the car door. "If Madame will honour me with her presence, I suggest we go and collect her things."

"Oh!" She put a hand to her mouth. "I nearly forgot. I've still got to tell Piers and Dennison! Oh, Julian, I'm not looking forward to it a bit."

"It'll soon be over," he said soothingly, "and anyway there's nothing they can do. You're not under contract, are you?"

"Yes, but I don't expect Dennison will hold me to it. He'll just make me feel like a worm for running out on him at such short notice." She slipped into the car and Julian got in beside her. "I think we'd better go to the theatre first."

"Shall I come in with you, darling?"

"No, thanks, I can manage."

"But if Dennison gets awkward –"

"Don't worry, it's too late for him to change my mind." She waved her left hand in front of her. "I'm Mrs. Summerford now."

"Mrs. Julian Summerford," he corrected gently.

For a moment she did not understand. Then: "Of course, Mrs. Summerford *junior*. But I'm still the happiest girl in the world!"

Only by an expressive shrug and curt dismissal did Dennison show her how deeply he was displeased. But Piers had no such inhibitions, and although Lucie had expected him to be angry she was taken aback by his vituperative reception of the news.

"Why the hell did you want to be a dancer in the first place if you were going to give it up to marry some Tom, Dick or Harry?"

"Julian's not just anybody, Piers. I never expected to get married, but I fell in love with him."

"In love! Ballet's your first and only love. If you don't know that now you ought to."

"You've no right to say that."

"And you've no right to walk out on me like this. What about my new ballet?"

"I'm sure Dennison's already made up his mind about it, so my leaving won't make any difference one way or the other.

Anyway, Adana will take over the part."

Piers flung away furiously. "Don't you realise I was trying to get Dennison to give it to you? Last night I even got him to say he'd consider it."

"Piers, you're joking!"

"Go and ask him if you don't believe me! We've worked so well together the last few months that I knew I'd found the right partner at last. Together we'd have gone to the top! Now you've made everything impossible."

She took a tentative step towards him. "I'm terribly sorry, Piers, but you'll succeed without me. Whether I'm here or not won't make any difference to that. I – I'll follow your progress, and get Julian to bring me to everything you do."

"Mother of God! After thirteen years' work do you have to be *brought*? If you wanted to get married so badly why couldn't you choose someone in the ballet?"

"Julian's very fond of it."

"*Fond* of it!" He lifted his hands in a gesture of contempt. "You talk as if it were a toy or a favourite food! And will his fondness for it make him the right husband for you – will it help him to understand that dancing is a part of your life?"

"It won't be a part of my life any more." Lucie's voice was firm. "I've no desire to make my dancing a bone of contention between Julian and me. For the past thirteen years my life has belonged to the practice-room and the stage and I don't intend to spend the rest of it in a world of unreality."

"So it's unreal all of a sudden?" Piers' face was tight. "And what about Pavlova and Karsavina – weren't they real?"

"You're defeating your own argument," she protested, "they were both married."

"I'm well aware of that. My whole point is that they married men who understood the ballet and wouldn't have dreamt of taking them away from it. If you had to get married, why didn't you marry me?"

"You? Really, Piers, I didn't think you'd go to the lengths of *marrying* a dancer to keep her as your partner. I'm sure there are lots of girls who'd be only too pleased to dance with you without your having to marry them."

Silently Piers turned away from the barre and sat down to unlace his pumps. "You over-estimate what I'd be prepared to do for the ballet, Lucie. However, you've obviously made up your mind, so there's no more to be said. You won't take any notice of me, so you must go your own way."

"Is that all you have to say?"

"What else do you expect? I'm afraid I can't offer my congratulations because the company's losing one of its potential ballerinas to become a suburban housewife."

"You rate me too high."

"On the contrary, you under-estimate yourself."

She moved towards the door.

"Lucie! Have you any idea what your life's going to be without dancing? If this man really loved you he wouldn't make you give it up."

She turned. "Julian isn't 'making' me do anything – I *want* to give it up. His work will take him abroad and we'd have no marriage if we were parted all the time."

Piers grunted. "I wouldn't want anyone to sacrifice their life to me."

"If you're in love it isn't a sacrifice."

"You think you know so much about love, don't you? When you've had time to think it over you'll bitterly regret what you're doing." He turned his back on her. "Remember the company's always here, Lucie – you may be glad of it one day."

CHAPTER III

BEING married to Julian was the most wonderful thing that had ever happened to Lucie and during their four months in Paris she was happier than she had ever been in her life. He was everything she had longed for in a lover – ardent, yet gentle and tender, subduing his passion to meet her own innocent desire.

Julian, too, was intensely happy, and every day found something new in Lucie to make him love her more, delighting in her quick changes of mood as she veered from seriousness to gaminerie. He had written to his mother as soon as they had arrived in Paris, and was eager to see her and make her understand that his love for Lucie had been so sudden in its development that it had swept aside all conscious deliberation or deceit.

Never had Paris seemed as lovely to him as it did now. It was as if he looked at everything through Lucie's wondering eyes, seeing for the first time the wide sweep of the Champs Elysées, the panorama of the city from the Eiffel Tower and the little restaurants where they shared such wonderful meals. She accepted all he bought for her with a delightful air of surprise, wringing the maximum of pleasure out of the most trifling gift.

Another thing that pleased him was her tacit acceptance of the long hours she had to spend alone while he was working at the Embassy, and when he returned would regale him with excited accounts of her visits to Notre Dame, the Sacré Coeur or the Louvre.

He expressed his relief at this one day and she looked at him in surprise. "But, Julian, it's your work. I couldn't expect you to stay with me all day."

He smiled. "I only thought you'd like me to be with you on our honeymoon."

"But it's your career, darling. Anyway, think how lucky we are that you were sent here in the first place. It'd be just as unthinkable for me to ask you not to go to work as – as–"

"As my asking you to give up the ballet?"

"That's different, Julian. I'm a woman, and as Byron said, 'Man's love is of man's life a thing apart, 'tis woman's whole existence'."

She was so sweetly solemn that he opened his arms and she flew into them. "Oh, Lucie, I love you so much! Don't ever change."

"As long as I can see my reflection in your eyes I never will."

All too soon Julian had to return to London and they spent their last evening at the Tour d'Argent, a restaurant high above the roof-tops of the city overlooking the Seine. Lucie wore one of the new dresses Julian had bought for her, and as she moved ahead of him to their table by the window she looked so much like a doll that he longed to pick her up in his arms and show her proudly to the world.

Choosing a meal was a ritual, and by the time they had eaten their pressed duck and crêpes suzettes the sky was dark and the lights of Paris twinkled below them like stars.

Lucie rested her head pensively on her hands and looked down at the river. "I shall miss all this when we go home."

"Never mind, sweetheart, we'll come back for a holiday."

"But holidays come every year and a honeymoon is over for ever."

"We'll make all our holidays honeymoons."

"I hope so, my darling. But this is the place where we've learnt to love each other and it can never be quite the same." She threw her arms wide in an expansive gesture. "Paris, city of love – how wonderful it sounds!"

He laughed and caught her hand. "And Rome and Washington and Madrid – wherever we're sent will be a city of love for us!"

They flew back to London late the following morning and to Julian's dismay Lucie was very air-sick. At Heathrow he saw her anxiously through the Customs to the car which was waiting for them, and she lay back against the seat too ill to speak. Far from wearing off, the sickness increased and he had to carry her through the lobby of the hotel where they were staying the night before going down to Devon.

Up in their room he laid her on the bed and looked down at her in concern. "This is more than just air-sickness, Lucie. I think you ought to have a doctor."

"Nonsense," she protested. "I'll be all right."

Reluctantly he agreed to wait, but even when she had slept for several hours she was still unwell and over-riding her protests he telephoned the hotel doctor.

He waited in the corridor while the man made his examination and looked at him anxiously as he came out of the bedroom.

"Nothing to worry about, Mr. Summerford. I've left your wife some pills and told her to take two with a cup of tea. She should feel better in the morning."

Julian went into the bedroom to find Lucie looking far more cheerful than he had expected.

He walked over and squeezed her hand. "I'm glad it's nothing serious, darling. The doctor says you'll be better in the morning."

"Perhaps, perhaps not."

"I'm sure you will, my love."

"On the contrary, I may be worse!"

He looked at her uncomprehendingly. Then something in her expression made him draw a sharp breath. "Lucie, you're not –?"

She nodded, her eyes shining. "Yes, darling, I am! We are!"

He caught her close and cradled her in his arms. "So a baby is going to have a baby! Oh, Lucie, how wonderful!"

She leaned back and looked up at him. "Are you really pleased, Julian? I mean, we haven't been married very long and we'll be tied down so much more."

"Of course I'm pleased, darling. I want a family and it doesn't matter to me how soon we start having one. I only want you to be well. That's the most important thing."

"Pouf, this is nothing! Now I know the reason for it I won't mind."

Contrary to her expectations, however, Lucie felt much better next morning and Julian decided to drive her down to Devon as planned. It was not until they were on the outskirts of London that she noticed the speedometer was barely touching twenty.

"Why are we going so slowly, Julian?"

"I thought speed might upset you – I must take extra care of you now."

"Silly old darling! Just because I'm going to have a baby doesn't mean I'm an invalid. I've told you before, you've got to be strong to be a ballet dancer."

"That was in the past."

"Even so, you needn't worry about me. I shall be the healthiest mother imaginable." She leant against him and yawned. "Let's have eight children, shall we?"

He laughed. "Not with income tax as high as it is! And I certainly don't want to lose sight of you in a welter of babies and nannies."

"Oh, I wouldn't like a nannie," she said quickly. "I want to look after my own baby. Nannies always seem to come between mothers and their children. It's not natural!"

He put an arm round her shoulders. "You can do anything you like, my darling, as long as you love me."

Lucie had never been to the West Country before and exclaimed delightedly at the terra-cotta earth and deep undulation of the countryside. But as they neared Shalford she began to fiddle nervously with her wedding-ring until at last Julian noticed it.

"What's the matter, darling, not feeling well again?"

"I feel all right, dear, it's just – I expect I'm afraid of meeting your mother."

He looked down at her in surprise, then drew the car to a standstill. "Whatever for, my love? I've never heard of anyone being afraid of Mother. She's the most understanding woman in the world."

"I'm sure she is," Lucie said quickly, "but will she like me? Won't she be resentful that you got married without telling her?"

"I can't imagine her ever being resentful, and anyway, as soon as she meets you, she'll understand why I did it."

Lucie pretended to be satisfied with this, but she could tell from his manner that Julian was almost as nervous as she was and longed for the meeting to be over, intensely curious to see the woman who could command such devotion in her son.

At the top of the hill he stopped the car for her to get her first view of Combe House, pointing it out through the trees.

"What a lovely place, Julian! I didn't know it was so big."

"I'm glad you like it, darling. It's our home."

She gave him a swift look but said nothing as they moved down the drive, glimpsing the sloping lawns that fell away to the sea. They drew up at the front door and it was opened almost immediately by a tall, well-built woman whom Lucie instantly recognised as her mother-in-law, for she had Julian's hair and the same easy grace of bearing.

"Julian, darling boy!" She came swiftly down the steps and Julian was out of the car to greet her before Lucie could move. Then he turned to his wife.

"Mother, this is Lucie."

Mrs. Summerford held out her hands. "It's so nice to meet you at last, my dear. I'm sure you must be tired after your long drive." She took the girl's arm and moved up the steps. "Don't bother about the cases, Julian, I'll get Gilchrist to bring them in."

Obediently Julian came up the steps and with an arm about each woman entered the house.

"My two favourite girls," he grinned. "Gosh, it's good to be home!"

During tea Mrs. Summerford questioned Julian about his work in Paris and Lucie relaxed and surveyed the lovely room with an observant eye. How graceful and elegant it was – and how large for one woman!

She looked up to see her mother-in-law's eyes on her. "Francis and Ann, my younger son and his wife, are coming over for dinner to meet you."

"That's nice," Lucie said warmly. "What a pity they don't still live here. Julian told me about it. This house must be very empty for you on your own."

A shadow crossed the calm face. "Mothers get used to being alone when their children grow up. It's one of the penalties of motherhood, my dear."

Lucie was conscious of Julian looking at her expectantly, but she said nothing.

Mrs. Summerford stood up. "When you've finished your tea I'll show you to your room."

"I'm ready now." Lucie put down her cup.

"There's no hurry, darling," Julian interposed. "I'll take you up in a minute. You needn't stand on ceremony with Lucie, Mother."

Mrs. Summerford smoothed her skirt. "Very well, dear. I've put you in the main bedroom."

"Your bedroom, you mean?"

"Of course. You're the master of the house, Julian, and now you're married it's only right that you and your wife should have it."

"I've no intention of taking it from you, Mother."

"Now, Julian dear, I've arranged everything. I assure you I'm quite comfortable in your old room."

Although Julian said no more, Lucie sensed that he was disturbed, and wondered why her mother-in-law had made such a point of giving them her bedroom when they would only be staying a few weeks.

The room proved to be large and airy, with a wide verandah that gave on to a magnificent view over the garden and sea. Lucie started to unpack, but Julian seemed ill at ease and moved around, lifting up and putting down the little ornaments and personal articles his mother had left on the mantelpiece and dressing-table.

He insisted on Lucie resting until dinner time and she lay on the bed after he had left the room, hearing the sea murmuring below as she dozed. At six o'clock she got up to change for her first evening at Combe House, and was tying the sash of her dress when there was a discreet tap at the door. She turned expectantly, thinking Julian had come to change for dinner. But it was her mother-in-law.

"Ah, you're up – I'm glad. Julian didn't want to disturb you so he's changing in the dressing-room next to my bedroom. I hope the journey didn't tire you too much?"

"Not at all, thank you."

"Good. I just came to tell you that dinner will be ready in about twenty minutes." For the first time she seemed to notice Lucie's dress. "Oh, what a pity, we were going to change for dinner tonight as it's a special occasion. A proper dinner-dress, I mean." She hesitated. "Oh well, never mind."

"Please, it's no bother," Lucie said quickly. "I can easily put on something else. Julian bought me a lovely dinner-dress in Paris and I'd like to wear it."

The woman smiled. "Perhaps it would be as well if you did. I want everything to be perfect for Julian's homecoming." She moved to the door. "See you downstairs, then, as soon as you're ready."

When Lucie went into the drawing-room it seemed to be full of people, but the minute Julian took her hand her nerves steadied and she saw that apart from Mrs. Summerford there were only two other men and a woman in the room.

Julian led her over to the tall, slim brunette sitting on the arm of the sofa.

"Lucie, this is my sister-in-law, Ann."

Ann's triangular face, with its generous mouth and deep-set eyes heavily made-up, crinkled into a smile as she extended her hand. In contrast to her somewhat artificial appearance her clasp was warm and natural.

"Hullo, Lucie. Welcome to the Summerfords."

"Don't forget me," a deep voice interrupted, and Francis Summerford bore down on her from the other side of the room. Slightly taller than Julian, he had none of his brother's close-knit vitality and seemed by comparison loosely built, his mouth more relaxed, his nose fleshier.

"What a nice sister-in-law!" He bent and kissed her heartily on the cheek. "Where did you find her, Julian – on top of a Christmas tree?"

Ann stubbed out her cigarette. "Don't mind my husband, Lucie, he's a natural buffoon."

Lucie glanced at her quickly, then smiled up at her brother-in-law. "We met at a cocktail party far too sophisticated to have anything as nice as a Christmas tree – and anyway, it wasn't Christmas!"

Francis grinned. "I always thought my brother had good taste."

The man standing by Ann's side came forward. "I'm not a Summerford myself, but I'd like to welcome you too. Congratulations, I hope you'll be very happy."

He was a stocky, erect man of about forty with a square, blunt face, vivid blue eyes surrounded by a network of fine lines and fair hair peppered with grey. "I'm an outsider," he went on, "so I can understand how overpowering it is to be plunged into a family you've never met before. Incidentally, I'm Simon

Hardy, Mrs. Summerford's estate manager."

"How do you do?" Lucie smiled. "Now I don't feel quite so shy."

"What about a drink?" Mrs. Summerford broke in. "Julian dear, will you do the honours?"

"Of course, Mother. Shall I mix some Martinis?"

"Yes, I think we all like them."

"Except Lucie," he replied as he went to the cocktail cabinet, "she prefers sherry."

At dinner Lucie sat between Francis and Simon Hardy with Ann and Julian opposite, while from the head of the table Mrs. Summerford conducted the flow of conversation. Sensitive to atmosphere, Lucie sensed an undercurrent of feeling between her mother-in-law and Ann and wondered whether the good-humoured Francis was as much aware of it as she was. But he did not seem to take any notice of his wife's acid remarks – indeed, whenever Ann addressed him it was in a scathing tone of voice, and looking across the table Lucie caught Julian's dark eyes fixed on her with such tenderness that she was thankful their own love was so full of understanding.

Coffee was served in the lounge and Simon Hardy came and sat next to her. She liked his unassuming personality and found him easy to talk to, wondering why Ann treated him with the same sharpness she used with all the Summerford family. Conversation was general for a while, but eventually Julian and Francis began to discuss the estate and although Lucie did her best to follow what was being said, the talk of crops and dairy yield failed to hold her interest, and at ten o'clock she stifled a yawn.

It did not escape her mother-in-law's sharp eyes. "Julian, Lucie's tired. You'd better see her up to bed."

"Yes, Mother." He stood up and held out his hand to Lucie who said her good nights with a murmur of apology. But as they reached the door Mrs. Summerford called again.

"Oh, Julian, you're not going to bed yet, are you? It's still quite early and there's so much I want to hear. I'm sure Lucie won't mind if you come down again – will you, Lucie dear?"

Lucie looked from her mother-in-law to her husband, but his face gave no sign of what he wanted to do and she murmured a polite negative as they left the room.

Upstairs in their bedroom Julian took her into his arms and rubbed his cheek against hers. "You don't mind if I go down again, do you, darling? I haven't seen Mother for such a long time."

She was touched by his half apologetic pleading. How like a little boy he was – eager to please two people at the same time without wanting to offend either of them!

"Of course I don't mind, darling. You must have a lot to tell your mother – but don't be too long."

"I won't."

He kissed her with a warmth that almost bespoke gratitude, and closed the door behind him.

Lucie opened her eyes next morning and stared up at the ceiling in perplexity. Then remembering where she was she looked across the room, surprised to see Julian's bed empty. Her watch showed nearly half past nine and she swung her legs out of the bed, hastily putting them back under the covers as there came a knock at the door and a young girl came in with a tray.

"Good morning, madam. Mrs. Summerford sent me up with your breakfast."

"Thank you. Would you put it on the other bed for me? I'll reach over and take it in a minute."

The girl obeyed and Lucie lay back and closed her eyes, opening them again to see Julian looking down at her, strangely unfamiliar in country tweeds.

"Morning, darling!" He bent and kissed her. "Sleep well?"

"Very." She held up her arms and pulled him down beside her. "You were up early – I didn't even hear you. Come and have breakfast with me."

"I've already had it."

"What a pity, I hate having it on my own."

"You were fast asleep when I dressed and I didn't want to disturb you. Anyway, I know you like breakfast in bed and Mother would have been disappointed if I hadn't had mine with her, especially the first morning. I always do when I'm home."

Lucie said nothing and Julian put the tray on her knees and went to the window, looking back at her as he sat down on the sill. "You know, it doesn't seem right our having this room.

I've always associated it with Mother."

She poured herself a cup of tea. "But it's the main bedroom and I expect she feels that now you're married –"

"That's got nothing to do with it." He spoke so sharply that she looked at him in surprise.

"I was only trying to appease your conscience, Julian."

"I know, darling. Forgive me. To tell you the truth I'm a bit on edge about Mother. She hasn't said a word about our getting married without telling her, and I don't like it."

"Perhaps there's nothing for her to say. After all, you're not a baby, Julian, and you didn't commit an unforgivable crime in marrying me."

Instantly he was by her side. "I didn't mean it that way, sweetheart. You know I'd marry you all over again if I had to."

She pulled him into her arms. "I should hope so, if only for the baby's sake!"

When he had gone Lucie bathed and dressed leisurely and went downstairs to find her mother-in-law crossing the hall. This morning, in the bright sunlight, she looked older and more lined, and impulsively Lucie went over and kissed her.

Mrs. Summerford drew back slightly and the girl's lips barely touched her cheek. "Good morning, my dear. I hope you slept well?"

"Very well, thank you." Lucie was conscious of having been rebuffed. "Where's Julian?"

"I think he's in the garden. I asked him to pick some flowers."

Lucie laughed. "I can't imagine Julian picking flowers!"

"Can't you? He's always done it for me, ever since he was a little boy." She moved into the drawing-room. "Come and sit down, my dear. I've hardly had time to talk to you since you arrived." Seating herself in an armchair, she picked up some knitting. "Tell me about yourself."

"There isn't much to tell. I'm twenty-three, my father was a doctor and I'm a ballet dancer, like my mother."

"You *are* a ballet dancer?"

Lucie flushed. "I mean I was. I've given it up."

"Naturally." The needles clicked. "I hope you don't mind my saying so, but you have rather an unusual appearance. Was your father a foreigner?"

"No, he was English. But my mother always referred to him as a foreigner because she was French!"

Mrs. Summerford reached the end of a row and turned. "I thought there was foreign blood somewhere in your family."

Lucie's eyes widened. "Do I look *so* unusual?"

"A little. That was probably your appeal for Julian. Men are always attracted by something different, don't you think? And then, of course, you've worked so many years with mixed nationalities."

"Oh no, Mrs. Summerford, they're all British."

"Indeed? I always thought ballet was something only foreigners went in for. Julian told me you were a nice little dancer."

Lucie smiled. "He's very tactful."

"I'm glad you appreciate that, Lucie. It isn't easy for a man to be tactful in a difficult situation."

"What's difficult, Mother?" They both looked up as Julian came into the room.

"Lucie and I were just talking about the ballet, darling. It all sounds most interesting. I do hope she won't miss it too much and want to go back."

Julian's eyes met Lucie's. "It'll be rather awkward if she does! As a matter of fact –"

"Will you show me the garden, darling?" Lucie stood up quickly. "I haven't seen it yet."

He looked surprised. "Yes, of course. We'll just have time before lunch. Incidentally, Ann rang up while you were dressing and asked us over for tea this afternoon."

"How nice of her." Lucie slipped her hand into his and they moved towards the french windows. "They've got a couple of children, haven't they?"

"Twins – Robert and Richard. They're panting to meet you." He halted suddenly and glanced round. "Come for a stroll, Mother?"

"No, dear, I'm sure you'd rather show Lucie the garden on your own. I'll wait for you here."

For an instant he hesitated, then with a slight smile drew Lucie out on to the terrace and across the lawn. As soon as they were out of earshot he slackened his pace. "Why didn't you want me to tell Mother about the baby, darling?"

"Oh, I don't know."

"Well, it's rather silly of you. She's sure to guess sooner or later and she'll be hurt if we don't tell her."

"I'm sorry. I didn't think. . . I just wanted to keep it to myself a little longer, that's all."

Instantly his frown disappeared. "What a child you are, I should have realised!"

After lunch they drove over to see Ann and Francis, and Lucie was charmed with the unpretentious cottage. As they stepped out of the car they heard the sound of children playing in the garden and before they were half-way up the front path two little boys came hurtling towards them and threw themselves on Julian.

He swung them up in his arms one after the other, then set them on their feet and turned them to face Lucie. They were pleasant-looking children with their mother's dark hair and Francis's square face and blue eyes.

"This is Robert and this is Richard, known locally as the 'terrible twins'! Boys, this is Aunt Lucie."

Lucie kissed them solemnly, wondering as she did so whether her own baby would look like them if it was a boy.

Talking and laughing, they entered a small, square hall gleaming with copper-ware and polished oak.

"Mummy's in here," Robert said, and led the way to the sitting-room. Ann rose to greet them. In a cherry red skirt and gaily embroidered blouse, her curly brown hair drawn back from her face with two combs, she looked younger and less sophisticated than the night before and Lucie wondered whether she had been wrong to dislike her.

"Hullo, you two! I wasn't sure you'd manage to get here."

"We had lunch rather late." Julian settled himself in an armchair. "Where's old Francis?"

"Somewhere around. I told him you were coming to tea so he'll probably be back about four." She went to the mantelpiece and took down a packet of cigarettes. "Smoke?"

Lucie shook her head, but Julian accepted one and Ann sat down again on the sofa and tucked her legs beneath her. "Well, Lucie, what do you think of Combe House?"

"It's lovely." Lucie spoke with genuine warmth. "But I like

your home just as much." She glanced round at the red-brick fireplace and hand-made rugs on the parquet floor. "Everything's so homely. It's furnished just the way a cottage ought to be."

"I'm glad you think so." Ann looked across at her brother-in-law. "What do you think of it, Julian – or don't you care to commit yourself?"

"It's very nice," he said equably, "but I still don't see why you had to leave Combe House."

"Because Mayfields is mine and Combe House is your mother's. Anyway, it's good for Francis to stand on his own feet and have the responsibility of a home, even if it's only a small one."

Julian's answer was forestalled by Francis's entry.

"Hullo, hullo, hullo!" Warm-heartedly he kissed Lucie s cheek. "How's Lucie Locket this afternoon?" Without waiting for a reply he flung himself into the armchair opposite Julian. "Mother all right? I haven't seen her today."

"She's fine."

"Good. I'll try and pop up this evening."

"She won't run away if you don't," Ann said sharply.

"Now, now, no quarrels in front of the newly-weds," Francis grinned. "Mustn't disillusion 'em too quickly!"

Ann stood up. "I'll go and get the tea."

"Let me help you." Lucie followed her into the compact little kitchen that looked out over the back garden. The tray had already been prepared and a plate of finely-cut bread and butter, a fruit cake and some Devonshire splits were waiting on the kitchen table.

"Did you do all this yourself?" she asked.

"Yes. My daily only stays till three and she's too busy washing-up to get tea. There's a lot to do with two kids, you know."

"I'm sure I couldn't manage half as well as you do."

"You won't *have* to manage if you don't want to."

"What do you mean?"

"The old girl'll foot your bills if you stay with her."

"I'm afraid there's not much likelihood of that." Lucie picked up the bread and butter. "Julian will be going abroad soon and I shall go with him."

"I wish to God Francis could be posted somewhere. I'd get him on his own then." Ann lifted the tray and kicked open the door.

Francis looked us as they entered. "I thought Simon was coming for tea?"

Ann put the tray on the gate-legged táble. "I didn't say anything to him about it last night. Did you?"

"No, but I mentioned it to him this morning." He turned to Julian. "Hardy's thinking of leaving, you know. He's been pretty restless for the last few months, so I wasn't altogether surprised when he asked me to try and find someone to take his place. I told him to think it over and let me know again at the end of the month, but I doubt if he'll change his mind."

"Bread and butter?" Ann proffered the plate.

Lucie took a slice. "I thought he was awfully nice. There's something rather sad about him."

"Funny how women go for the spaniel look, isn't it?" Francis grinned at his brother.

"He ought to get married," Julian rejoined. "I can recommend it."

"Recommend what?" a clipped voice demanded, and they looked round to see Simon Hardy stepping through the french windows.

The twins jumped up and threw themselves at him. "Just in time for tea, Uncle Simon, just in time for tea!"

"We were trying to marry you off," Julian called through the pandemonium.

The man advanced into the room with the two little boys clinging to him. "Who to?"

"Hadn't got around to that yet," Francis said. "We'll let you know when we do."

"I don't suppose you've had tea, have you?" Ann spoke with familiar sharpness.

"No, I'd love some. But don't get up, I'll help myself."

"Nonsense," she said ungraciously, and got up to do it for him, handing him his cup before she sat down again to supervise the children. "Richard, you're not to have another cake until you've eaten some bread and butter."

"I'm not hungry for bread and butter," the little boy said, solemnly filling his mouth with Devonshire split.

"If you're hungry for cake you're hungry for bread and butter."

"No, I'm not."

"I'm not either," Robert chimed in.

For the first time Lucie saw a smile in Ann's eyes. "Well, if you're sick don't blame me." She turned to Lucie. "Like some more tea?"

"Please."

"What about staying for supper? We've got plenty of food."

"What a good idea! Can we, Julian?"

In earnest conversation with Francis, Julian looked up. "Can we what?"

"Stay to supper?"

" 'Fraid not, darling. Mother's expecting us."

Ann shrugged. "Never mind, Lucie, perhaps you can come over on your own one evening."

"I'd love to."

Julian glanced at his watch. "That reminds me, we'd better be going. I promised we wouldn't be late."

As Julian spoke Lucie was conscious of Ann's cynical amusement, and for the first time felt like arguing with him. Did he always have to obey his mother's wishes? Didn't he have any mind of his own? But as soon as they had driven out of sight of Mayfields Julian took her in his arms and she forgot her annoyance in the rapture of his kisses.

The first month at Combe House passed in an easy, pleasant routine. Lucie continued to have breakfast in her room and did not go downstairs until mid-morning, when Julian was usually out on the estate with his mother. In the afternoon Mrs. Summerford rested and Lucie had her husband to herself. She looked forward to these hours most of all, and counted the days until they would be returning to London and a home, however small, of their own. But although she longed to leave Devon, the indolent life suited her, and she began to relax and lose some of the quick tensity of a dancer. Her skin browned easily and her pale, colourless hair was bleached by the sun. She had still not told her mother-in-law she was expecting a baby, and although she knew it was often on the tip of Julian's tongue to do so she was glad he respected her desire to keep their secret.

Mrs. Summerford's attitude remained graciously cool and Lucie felt none of the warmth she had expected to feel for Julian's mother. After that first morning she had never attempted to kiss her again and was embarrassed one evening when Mrs. Summerford asked why she never did so. Julian's face tightened and Lucie hurried across the room to place her lips against her mother-in-law's smooth cheek, hoping to pass the incident off as lightly as possible. But on the way up to bed he remarked on it.

"Mother's very sensitive, you know, and Francis and I have always tried to make up for the fact that Father died when we were so young."

"I didn't think she'd like me to kiss her," Lucie said awkwardly.

"You think about things too much, dear. That sort of gesture should come spontaneously. Mother says –" He checked himself abruptly.

"What does she say?"

He hesitated for a moment. "Mother thinks you're rather self-contained."

He moved ahead to open the bedroom door and did not notice the hurt expression on her face.

"Do *you* think I'm self-contained, Julian?"

"Not as far as I'm concerned, darling, but then other people don't see you the way I do."

"I'm not concerned with other people," she retorted sharply. "I'm only concerned with you, and as long as I do what you like –"

"Well, I'd like to feel that Mother loves you as much as I do."

Lucie sat down on the bed and looked up at him. "I think you're expecting an awful lot, darling. After all, your mother and I haven't known each other long."

"That's got nothing to do with it. After all, it's only natural for you to love Mother and for her to love you. Why make something complex out of a perfectly normal relationship?"

He looked so confident of his assertion and so genuinely perturbed that she had not the heart to contradict him, and held out her arms. "Oh, Julian, you're so sweet and I love you for it!"

Instantly he went to her. "And I love you. Lucie, love, don't let's quarrel."

They had been at Combe House five weeks when Julian received notice from the Foreign Office to report for details of his new posting, and travelled up to London the following day.

Without him the house seemed bigger than ever and Lucie stayed in her room as long as possible, unable to rid herself of a feeling of uneasiness.

When she went downstairs her mother-in-law was arranging flowers in the drawing-room and received her dutiful morning kiss with the usual lack of response.

"Good morning, Lucie. I hope you slept well."

Always the same question, always the same answer. "Very well, thank you, Mother." It was an effort to call her this, remembering her own impulsive, warm-hearted mother, but for Julian's sake she did so. "Can I help you with the flowers?"

"No, thank you, dear." The capable hands placed another tulip in the bowl. "I know just how they should go. Julian doesn't like too many in a vase, he says it spoils the line."

"Julian has a good eye for line. Perhaps that's why he likes the ballet."

Her mother-in-law pursed her lips. "I suppose so. But most young men seem to like the theatre in one form or another until they grow out of it."

"Sometimes the liking lasts all their lives."

"I think that depends on the man, although I suppose pretty young performers always hold a certain appeal. That's something divorced from reality about them."

Lucie's mouth tightened. "There are quite a number of successful women on the stage who are neither young nor pretty."

"If you're referring to actresses, my dear, they hardly have the same sort of audience as a chorus girl."

"Many stars have risen from the ranks of the chorus," Lucie said coldly. "There's no shame in that."

The plump shoulders lifted. "You're much more knowledgeable about it than I am, of course, I'm afraid I've always led a very sheltered life. The Summerford men have never liked their wives to have careers."

"Then Julian must be different."

"In what way? Didn't he insist on your giving up your career as soon as you were married?"

"Yes, but only because he knew he'd be sent abroad."

"Even if Julian remained in England I don't think he'd want you to go on dancing. Men in his position have to be so careful."

"Really, Mrs. Summerford, you talk as if being in the ballet was a disgrace!"

"Mrs. Summerford?" The round face was distressed. "I thought you were going to call me Mother."

Lucie bit her lip. "I'm sorry, it slipped out."

"Never mind, it's quite understandable. After all, we haven't known each other very long."

Lucie forced a smile and wondered how her mother-in-law always managed to put the other person in the wrong.

"Do you know very much about the Diplomatic Corps, Lucie?"

"No, I'm afraid not."

"What a pity. I always think a wife can be so helpful to her husband. Still, no doubt you'll learn."

"I'm sure I shall, Mother. But surely a man can get on in his career without his wife?"

"What an odd point of view, my dear – I suppose that's your foreign outlook."

Lucie controlled herself. "I didn't mean I wouldn't help him – it's just that Julian doesn't strike me as needing anyone's support."

"How little you know him! Although he may seem independent he's always relied on me more than he realises."

"Do you think it's fair to let someone rely on you so much?"

"Of course! That's what a mother's for."

"But surely there comes a time when a son ceases to be a child, and the more he relies on his mother the harder he'll find the transition. I shall encourage my children to be independent from the start."

"Then, if you'll permit me to say so, you'll be depriving them of the security they need and have a right to expect from you."

"They'll still have the security of my love without the need of being propped up!"

Mrs. Summerford smiled. "When you have children of your

own you'll realise that's easier said than done."

After this, conversation languished, and presently Lucie excused herself and went out into the garden where she wandered disconsolately until lunch. The two women ate together in the breakfast-room overlooking the sweep of hills behind the house. Even in the intimacy of this little room Mrs. Summerford managed to remain impressive and unapproachable, investing her every action with majesty, and Lucie thought she had never met anyone more careful of what she said and did, making it almost impossible to feel at ease with her. Yet how could she explain this to Julian when there was nothing specific with which to find fault?

In the afternoon Mrs. Summerford went to her room to rest and Lucie was left to her own devices. She had tea in the drawing-room, and felt so lonely that she was almost tempted to go into the kitchen and have it with the housekeeper. But her mother-in-law discouraged any familiarity with the servants, and she remained in the room on her own, a small, solitary figure on the large tapestry couch.

At five o'clock she began to listen for Julian's car and went to the window several times thinking she heard it. But six o'clock arrived and he had still not returned and she ran upstairs to change, hoping a different dress would make her feel more cheerful.

As she opened the wardrobe door the full-length mirror reflected the slight thickening of her waist and hips, the fuller curve of her bosom. She would not be able to keep her secret very much longer and felt an excited longing to hold her baby in her arms. Would it be a boy or a girl? Would it have Julian's eyes and her hair or would it look like her own mother – or even his?

She reached into the wardrobe and at the same time heard the sound of Julian's car coming up the drive. In a couple of minutes she would be in his arms again, and nothing else mattered.

But she had finished changing and was at the mirror doing her hair before he came into the room.

"Hullo, sweetheart." He kissed the nape of her neck. "What a long day it's been without you!"

She turned in his arms. "You've been home over a quarter

of an hour, darling. Where have you been?"

"Talking to Mother. She was just coming downstairs as I came in."

Lucie bit her lips on a sharp retort. He looked so tired that she didn't want to quarrel with him. "What's the news of your posting?"

He sat down on the bed and took off his jacket, loosening his collar and tie. "It seems I'll be staying in London for quite a while yet – at least six months, I should think." He sprawled back on the bed. "Lord, I'm fagged. Be thankful you didn't go with me, Lucie. It was baking in town." She perched on the bed by his side and he caught her hand and played with her fingers. "Had a nice day, darling? I was envying you down here."

"It was lonely without you."

"You had Mother."

"She went up to rest after lunch and I haven't seen her since."

"That's funny. She seemed to think you didn't want to be with her. That's why she didn't come down for tea."

"There was no question of my not wanting to be with her," Lucie protested. "On the contrary, I thought she didn't want to be with me."

He nuzzled against her shoulder. "Why should you think that, silly baby?"

"Because your mother and I had a – a little discussion about the theatre this morning. I must say she seems to have some very odd ideas about it, Julian. I got the impression that she doesn't approve of my having been a dancer."

"Nonsense, it's just that she's a bit old-fashioned. Mother always admits she's led a very sheltered life."

"Not every woman can afford to," Lucie said sharply.

"Hey, hey!" He pulled her against him. "Is my little kitten getting her claws out? You musn't take everything Mother says so seriously. You know she wouldn't knowingly do anything to upset you."

Lucie kissed his cheek and moved back to the dressing-table. "I suppose you're right. It's just that your mother isn't used to sharing her home with another woman."

"That's hardly true, darling. Ann lived here for several years."

"Even so, it'll be better when we have a home of our own, and now you know you'll be staying in England we can look for a flat."

Julian's reply was cut short by the sound of the dinner gong and with a hurried: "I'd better wash or the dinner'll get spoilt," he disappeared into the bathroom.

At dinner that evening Lucie made a determined effort to be pleasant.

"Isn't it nice that Julian's going to stay in England, Mother?"

"From my point of view it is, but I can't help thinking he'd get more useful experience if he were posted abroad."

Lucie wondered exactly what her mother-in-law really did want. "Well, it's better for us to be in England for the time being." She glanced at Julian and he nodded with a quick smile. "We've got something to tell you, Mother. I'm going to have a baby."

Mrs. Summerford's coffee spoon fell with a clatter and she bent to pick it up. "Congratulations, my dear. How nice for you. When is it to be?"

"In about six months."

"So soon?"

"We didn't see any reason to wait."

Mrs. Summerford flushed. "I didn't mean that – I would never presume to interfere in something so personal. I only meant that I'm surprised you've known for so long without telling me."

"Lucie wanted to keep it to herself, Mother," Julian interposed.

"How strange! When I was going to have a baby I was so pleased I wanted everyone to know. But there, we're not all alike." She reached out and patted Lucie's hand. "I hope you don't mind too much?"

"Mind? I'm thrilled!"

"I'm so glad. I thought perhaps you might not have wanted a baby so soon. After all, you've led such an active life you'll probably find it more difficult than most women to settle down to motherhood."

"Considering I gave up my career to get married, I don't think so." Lucie stood up. "Now if you'll excuse me, I'm going to bed."

"Of course, my dear." Mrs. Summerford held up her cheek and with an effort Lucie bent to kiss it.

"Will you be long, Julian?" she asked.

"No, I'll be up before you're asleep."

The door closed behind her and Julian sighed.

"Don't look so stern, darling," Mrs. Summerford said gently.

"Was I, Mother? To tell you the truth, I'm a bit annoyed with Lucie."

"There's no need to be. She's very young and rather unimaginative, that's all."

"But that's just it – if she really *was* unimaginative I could understand it. But she isn't. She's too intelligent for that."

"I'm sure she is, dear, but you must make allowances for her. After all, she hasn't had much time to settle down and I expect she's still a little overwhelmed by everything. And now this wonderful new experience has come along when she's probably not quite ready to meet it."

"What do you mean? I've always thought Lucie wanted the baby."

"Then she's more sensible than I imagined. She probably realises it'll help her forget the ballet."

Julian played with his coffee cup. "Do you think she does miss it? She never says anything to me."

"Perhaps not, but little things she's let drop make me think she does. Still, as long as we know, we can guard against it and make sure she doesn't brood. I did my best this morning, although I'm afraid I didn't succeed very well." She smiled slightly. "But now I know her condition it explains a great deal. Many women get fanciful with a first baby and we must just make allowances for her."

Julian leaned over and touched his mother's hand. "Darling Mother, thank you for being so understanding."

Going downstairs a few days later, Lucie was surprised to see Ann walking up the drive with the twins. Francis was a daily visitor, but Ann had not set foot in the house since the evening of their arrival, and Lucie hurried down to meet her.

"Hullo, Ann, how are you?"

"Fine. I wondered whether you'd still be here."

"We wouldn't go without saying good-bye to you."

Ann gave a brief smile. "Where's the old girl?"

"Going round the estate with Julian."

"Lord, how familiar that sounds!"

Without replying Lucie led the trio out on to the terrace.

"Can we go and play down by the pool?" Richard asked.

"Yes, if you're careful not to fall in."

The two little boys ran off and Lucie watched until they were out of sight before she settled into a deck chair by Ann's side.

Her sister-in-law lit a cigarette. "Seriously, how long do you and Julian intend staying here?"

Lucie shrugged. "We'll have to find a furnished flat before we can leave here. Are they difficult to get?"

"Not if you can afford to pay a decent rent."

"Good. I want to get settled before the – I'm expecting a baby, you know."

Ann whistled. "Do I offer congratulations or condolences? Does the old girl know?"

"Yes."

"It must have spiked her guns."

Lucie leant forward. "Why do you dislike her so much?"

"It's a long story," Ann said drily. "Remind me to tell it to you one day. How's she been behaving?"

"I think she finds it difficult to realise that Julian's married."

"I'm not surprised. She hasn't realised Francis is yet. Take warning from me, Lucie, before it's too late. Whatever you do, make her understand that you're Julian's wife and you come first."

"Of course I come first! Surely there's no need to point that out?"

Ann grunted. "Your innocence may defend you. I only hope that if you can't learn by someone else's mistakes you don't have to learn by your own." She craned her neck. "Here she comes now, clutching on to Julian as if she couldn't walk without him!"

Lucie followed her gaze to where Mrs. Summerford and Julian were strolling across the lawn. Every now and then they stopped to admire a clump of flowers and Lucie felt a spasm of irritation that Julian did not come straight up once he had seen Ann. Surely he knew the garden well enough not to have to gape at it all over again?

"Julian!" she called.

He lifted his hand and waved, but made no move to join them.

"The mater might fall down without his support – she's so frail, you know," Ann said mockingly, and for once Lucie appreciated her sarcasm.

A few moments later Julian and his mother came on to the terrace. "Good afternoon, Ann," Mrs. Summerford said graciously. "You haven't been to see us for a long while."

"Ah, but you've got someone to take my place, Mother. Anyway, I've been busy."

"I suppose Mayfields does take a good deal of your time. Still, I get all the news from Francis." She sat down on a deck chair Julian placed for her. "You know, dear, I wouldn't bother to give him sandwiches every day. It's such a waste when he can eat here. By the way, I hope you don't mind, but I've sent the children in to have their tea. We met them by the pool."

Angry colour flooded into Ann's face. "I do mind! I wanted them to have it out here with us."

"Oh dear, now I've done the wrong thing again."

Julian breached the uncomfortable silence. "Is Francis coming to take you home or did you bring the car?"

"No, we walked over."

"Then I'll run you back myself when you're ready."

"Thanks." The flush ebbed slowly and Ann relaxed uneasily in her chair. "Lucie's been telling me you're going back to London soon."

"Yes, I'll be there for several months yet. Has she told you our other news?"

"About the baby, you mean? Yes. Congratulations. You'll have to find a flat with a garden."

He smiled. "Later, perhaps. For the moment I think it would be better if Lucie stayed down here."

Lucie sat up straight. "I've no intention of being parted from you!"

"I'll be down every weekend, darling, and the country's much healthier for you now."

"But Julian, I thought we'd decided –"

"I think it'd be better if you didn't have the bother of flat-hunting and running a home," he persisted.

Lucie trembled with sudden anger. "Really, Julian, you talk as if I were an invalid! If I was strong enough to be a dancer I'm quite strong enough to have a baby and run a flat like thousands of other women."

"But, my dear, why do it when there's no need?" Mrs. Summerford put in mildly.

"There's every need!" Lucie rejoined. "I want to be with Julian and I want a home of my own. Besides, we should be together at a time like this."

"We *will* be, darling," Julian said placatingly. "I've already told you I'll be down every weekend."

"You've got it all worked out, haven't you?" she rounded on him. "Is there anything else you've decided without consulting me? Or perhaps you haven't quite forgotten that marriage is supposed to be a partnership?"

"Really, Lucie, you're being most unreasonable. I only suggested –"

"Julian dear," Mrs. Summerford interrupted, "don't lose your temper. Lucie's overwrought and excited."

"I'm not overwrought or excited," Lucie flared. "And I wish you'd mind your own business!"

"How dare you speak to Mother like that!" Julian said angrily. "She's only trying to –"

"She's trying to separate us!" Lucie cried. "Can't you see that, or are you blind?" She flung away and slammed the drawing-room door behind her, ignoring Julian's cry of "Lucie!" as she ran across the room.

"Well, well," Mrs. Summerford said disapprovingly, "I must say I never thought Lucie would behave *quite* so badly. As if we weren't suggesting everything for her own good . . ."

Ann stubbed out her cigarette viciously. "Haven't you done Francis and me enough harm without trying to come between Julian and Lucie?"

Julian's lips tightened. "You've no right to talk to Mother like that. She's had quite enough to put up with from you already."

"What do you think I've put up with from her for the last six years?"

He stood up. "I'll see you home, Ann. You'd better go and fetch the children while I bring the car round."

When he had gone Mrs. Summerford folded her hands. "You've only yourself to blame if you're not happy, Ann. You knew when you married Francis that his life was down here."

"I knew his life was down here, but I thought it would belong to me, not to his mother!"

Mrs. Summerford rose. "I've been very patient with you, but this time I think you've gone too far. When you first came here as Francis's fiancée I told you he was a weak man. If you wanted a more forceful husband you should have taken my advice and broken your engagement."

Ann's nostrils dilated. "You'd have liked that, wouldn't you? But you reckoned without one thing – I loved Francis when I married him, and I married him because I thought he needed me."

"He had me."

"And you still have him, you'll be pleased to know! If it weren't for the children you could have him back altogether."

"A mother is always ready to take her sons back. It's a love that doesn't change when other loves have failed them."

Ann walked over to the french windows and turned with her hand on the knob. "If I wrote a book about my life here I'd call it *The Stranglehold*. It would be a psychological study of a woman who destroyed her own children!"

The dark eyes flickered. "I don't think you'll be very welcome here in future."

"I don't think I'll want to be!"

Julian was waiting in the car with the twins and opened the door as Ann appeared. They were out of sight of the house before he spoke, lowering his voice so that the children should not hear.

"You really should learn to control your temper, Ann, for Francis's sake if not your own."

"Perhaps one day you'll realize how much I've put up with for Francis's sake! Anyway, it doesn't matter any more."

"That's a childish thing to say."

"It's equally childish to bury your head in the sand!" Ann looked at her brother-in-law earnestly. "I'm fond of you, Julian, or I wouldn't have said what I did. For God's sake don't let your marriage go like mine! Lucie's a sweet girl and she loves you, but I won't answer for her if she has to go through six years like I've had."

"The question won't arise. I've no intention of letting Lucie get as out of hand as Francis has let you!"

"Good heavens, Julian, wives aren't meant to be kept in check, like dogs on the lead! You're not weak like Francis, but you're not naturally autocratic either – it's just something you've absorbed from your mother. Once you begin making decisions without consulting Lucie you're heading for the rocks – you've got to talk things over with your *wife*, not your mother. It's your duty as a husband."

"I'm surprised you use the word duty. From the way you've been talking today I wouldn't have thought it existed in your vocabulary. But it isn't only husbands and wives who have a duty to each other, sons and daughters have a duty to their parents, and one tie is just as strong as the other."

Ann shrugged. "As long as you go on thinking like that, it's no good discussing it. I shan't be seeing very much of you from now on, Julian, but one day you'll remember what I've said and I hope it won't be too late when you do."

Julian made no reply and they finished the journey in silence, the awkwardness of parting glossed over by the presence of the children.

Back at Combe House Lucie heard Julian and Ann drive off and sat up to dry her eyes. Mayfields was only a few miles away and Julian would soon be back. She was already beginning to feel ashamed of her outburst and waited nervously for him to return. Fifteen minutes passed, then twenty and twenty-five, and there was still no sign of him. Agitatedly she paced the room but when an hour had elapsed she could bear it no longer and hurried downstairs.

She had reached the hall when the telephone rang and she went across and picked up the receiver. A male voice asked to speak to Mrs. Summerford.

"This is Mrs. Julian Summerford speaking. Can I help you?"

"Teincombe General Hospital here, Mrs. Summerford. Your husband's just been brought in. His car overturned on the Shalford road about half an hour ago."

All the strength seemed to ebb out of Lucie's body. "Is he –

is he badly hurt?"

"Nothing very serious," the man replied, "a couple of broken bones and some bruises. If you come along later this evening we'll be able to give you more details."

"I see. Thank you." She replaced the receiver and closed her eyes, steadying herself against the wall. The vision of Julian lying hurt and unattended on some lonely road was agonizing and she longed to run to him. Terrible to believe they had parted in anger!

Coming downstairs a few moments later Mrs. Summerford paused at the sight of the still figure in the hall below her.

"What's the matter, Lucie? Aren't you well?"

Lucie looked up. "It isn't me, Mother, it's Julian."

"Julian? What's the matter with him?" The woman came down the last flight of stairs precipitately. "Tell me, quickly – what's the matter with him?"

"He's had an accident in the car – they've taken him to Teincombe Hospital."

"Is he seriously hurt? Will he be all right? For goodness' sake pull yourself together and answer me!"

Lucie moistened her lips. "They couldn't tell me much. They – I – I don't think it was a doctor speaking. The man said a couple of bones were broken."

"Think? Don't they know? Why didn't you call me to the phone?"

"They asked to speak to me."

Mrs. Summerford gave an exclamation of impatience and went to the telephone. "Go and sit in the drawing-room – I'll be in in a minute."

Numbly Lucie did as she was told and a few moments later her mother-in-law came into the room.

"I've spoken to the doctor in charge and he says Julian's just been X-rayed. By the time we get to the hospital they should have the result. Run upstairs and put on your coat and we'll go right away."

At the hospital a nurse led them into a small waiting room where they were joined almost immediately by the doctor. He obviously knew Mrs. Summerford well, for he shook her hand and smiled reassuringly. "Now there's no cause for alarm, Mrs.

Summerford – a broken ankle and a fractured collar-bone. It could have been much worse."

"Thank God it wasn't. To think that he was perfectly all right a few hours ago." She sank on to a chair and wiped her eyes, then as an afterthought turned to Lucie. "Oh, Lucie, this is Dr. Christy. He's known Julian since he was a little boy. Doctor, this is Julian's wife."

Dr. Christy eyed Lucie professionally. "You look all in, my dear. I think I'll give you a sedative."

"Please don't bother, thank you. I just want to see Julian."

"I'm afraid you both can't go in to see him tonight. He's suffering from shock and I don't want him excited."

Mrs. Summerford stood up. "Don't you think I'd better go, Lucie? You may get distressed and it won't do you or Julian any good."

"I'll be perfectly all right, thank you, Mother."

"I honestly don't think you should, my dear. Now do be guided by me. Stay here and let the doctor give you a sedative and I'll come straight back."

"I want to see Julian myself." Lucie turned to the doctor who was looking fixedly at the floor. "Please take me to my husband, Dr. Christy."

Lucie knew it would be a long time before she would get the memory of Julian's white face out of her mind. Although he was barely conscious when she kissed him she was sure from the faint response of his lips that he recognised her. But there was nothing she could do or say and when she had sat with him for a few minutes he drifted off into complete unconsciousness and she crept out of the room.

They drove back to Combe House in silence. Mrs. Summerford was frigid, but Lucie saw no reason to apologise. As Julian's wife she had been entitled to see him – indeed a hospital always gave preference to a wife or husband, and if Dr. Christy had not known the family this unpleasantness need never have arisen.

Throughout dinner Mrs. Summerford maintained her air of grievance, and Lucie excused herself as soon as they had finished coffee and went upstairs to bed. Alone in her room the realisation of Julian's accident was even more acute and she kept visualising his face on the hospital pillow. Would he have asked to see her or his mother if he had had the choice? She tossed restlessly, searching for the answer, but none came and at last she fell into a troubled, fitful sleep.

It was nearly ten o'clock when she awoke and she wondered what had happened to her breakfast tray. Hurriedly she washed and dressed and went down to the kitchen.

Gladys was setting the tray and looked up in surprise.

"Good morning, Mrs. Julian. I was just coming up."

"Why are you so late, Gladys?"

"Mrs. Summerford told me not to disturb you, madam. She said you were upset by poor Mr. Julian's accident and needed a good long sleep, so I was to let you lie."

"That was kind of her. Is she still in her room?"

"Oh no, Mrs. Julian, she went to the hospital ages ago."

"You mean she's there already?"

"Yes, madam. She rang up only a few minutes back to say she's bringing Mr. Julian home with her. Now would you like me to put your breakfast tray in the dining-room?"

"No, thank you. I only want a cup of coffee."

Lucie went across the hall with the cup in her hand and sat down at the dining-room table. Sipping the coffee absent-mindedly she pondered her mother-in-law's behaviour. Surely there had been no need for such secrecy? Even if Mrs. Summerford wanted to exercise her right as Julian's mother it was undignified and deceitful to have gone to the hospital without his wife's knowledge.

She was on her way upstairs to fetch her coat when there was the sound of cars in the drive. Hurriedly she ran down again to see an ambulance and Mrs. Summerford's car drawn up at the front door and two attendants manoeuvring a stretcher out of the back. Lucie went down the steps and bent over Julian.

His colour was better today, although his face was still drawn, the thick bandages around his shoulder giving him a distorted, top-heavy appearance.

"Hullo, darling – fine one I am, giving you such a fright!"

"Oh, Julian, thank God you're home." Tears started into her eyes. "I didn't think they'd let you leave so soon."

He grinned weakly. "You know what Mother is when she gets going."

Mrs. Summerford smiled gently. "It was nothing, darling. I

only insisted because I knew you'd be more comfortable at home. Now, Lucie, you're holding up the ambulance men. We must get Julian to bed as quickly as possible."

"I'm sorry." Lucie moved away. "I'll go ahead and see that the bed is ready."

"There's no need for that, dear. Julian will go in Francis's old room till he's better. It's always used as the sick-room in emergencies."

In silence Lucie watched her husband carried upstairs, too thankful that he was safe to object at the way her mother-in-law had taken everything into her own hands.

If Lucie had been less charitable she could almost have thought that her mother-in-law enjoyed Julian's illness, for his dependance and need of attention seemed to give her immense satisfaction and she refused to engage a nurse, insisting on doing everything for him herself.

"But, Mother, it's far too much for you," Lucie protested. "You'll wear yourself out if you keep running up and down the stairs all day."

"I don't notice it, Lucie."

"But I want to take up Julian's trays myself and make him the special little dishes he likes."

"That's not necessary, dear. Gladys is quite used to cooking for him and she knows all his favourite recipes."

"But there must be something I can do for him," Lucie burst out.

Mrs. Summerford laid a hand on her arm. "In your condition, the less you do the better."

"*I'm* not the invalid, Mother – having a baby is a perfectly natural function and if I haven't anything to occupy me, the next few months are going to be far more tedious."

"Poor Lucie, I'm sorry you find it tedious having a baby."

"I didn't say that! I only meant –"

"I know what you mean, but you shouldn't do anything to upset yourself, even if the time does hang heavy. I quite understand you want to do little things for Julian, but believe me, you'll be helping yourself if you don't."

Lucie was not deceived by this line of argument, but she said nothing more and hovered at the foot of the stairs the whole of the morning. It was nearly half-past twelve before her mother-in-law came into view carrying Julian's luncheon tray from the kitchen.

Lucie darted across the hall. "I'll take that up, Mother."

The plump face hardened. "I thought we decided you weren't going to run up and down stairs."

"*You* decided, I didn't." And without more ado Lucie took the tray and walked upstairs.

Thus began a series of tussles between the two women; a conflict that developed entirely without Julian's knowledge. Lucie had hoped that once Mrs. Summerford realised she had made up her mind to look after her husband herself she would give way gracefully, but her mother-in-law seemed completely impervious to the fact that each argument was a repetition of the last, and four or five times a day Lucie had to brace herself for the inevitable clash. But the more persuasive Mrs. Summerford was the more determined Lucie became, and although each encounter was a quiet one it left her nervously exhausted.

Julian's accident had left the quarrel between them unresolved, for there was no question of his returning to London for at least two months. Over and over again she asked herself whether she was in any way to blame – whether his preoccupation with her had caused the accident – and he seemed to sense what was going through her mind, for one afternoon when they were alone together he mentioned it.

Lucie was sitting miserably by the window while outside the trilling notes of a bird sounded against the murmur of the sea.

"Come here, my darling," he said softly.

She saw his hand outstretched and in an instant was at his side, kneeling on the floor by the bed with tears pouring down her cheeks.

"Now then, what's all this about? Not blaming yourself for my accident, by any chance?"

"Oh, Julian, I can't help thinking it was all my fault! If only I hadn't –" She broke off on a sob, and he cradled her head in the crook of his arm.

"You poor little darling, I had a feeling you were blaming yourself. Lucie, look at me."

She raised her head and he was filled with compassion at the sight of her tear-stained face. How incredible it was that this child-like creature was bearing his child! With infinite tenderness he ran a finger across her cheek and wiped the tears away.

"An accident can happen to anyone, darling. No matter how careful you are you can't always make allowances for the other fellow."

"If I hadn't upset you you might have been able to avoid it."

"That doesn't say very much for my driving," he joked. "Anyway, you mustn't think I'm going to take every silly little quarrel so much to heart. It was bad luck, but at least it'll keep me down here with you a bit longer, so try and see the good side of it."

With an effort she controlled an impulse to reopen the argument. Time enough for that when he was well again.

Although Lucie spent all day with Julian it was at night that she missed him most. The sick-room was directly opposite her mother-in-law's bedroom and she tentatively suggested that Mrs. Summerford move back into her old room and allow her to occupy the one near Julian. But this was met with such a stony expression that she had not ventured to pursue the subject.

Julian's illness gave Francis a further excuse to remain at Combe House and he lunched there every day, quite often returning for dinner. His mother made no move to send him home and Lucie was curious to know what they found to discuss at such length, and wondered if he ever gave a thought to Ann sitting alone in the house she had hoped would bring them closer together.

The sick-room routine continued monotonously, and one afternoon she slipped on a loose coat, changed into a pair of walking shoes and set off in the direction of Mayfields. At the end of the drive she looked back towards her husband's bedroom and Mrs. Summerford waved graciously from the window. Lucie waved back with a smile of ironic amusement. Her mother-in-law must have gone up as soon as she knew Julian was alone. With a metaphoric shrug she set off down the winding road into Shalford..

She walked through the village square with its bowling green and sedate patch of gardens, past the village inn with the painted sign, and out along the motor road the other side. The ascent soon became steep and several times she paused to rest.

How ridiculous to be tired and short of breath – she who had been able to practise for four and five hours at a time and then give a performance in the evening! She loosened her coat and there was a flutter beneath her ribs, a little tremor of movement so faint that it passed almost unnoticed. Suddenly she was aware of the miracle taking place within her – a miracle that would continue no matter what happened in her outward life. Here was something that would go on undisturbed by quarrels and conflict, a steady progress towards fulfilment that remained isolated from everything outside. Feeling the life stir within her she laughed at herself for ever believing that Mrs. Summerford could come between her and Julian while she was bearing his child. At that moment he seemed to belong to her more completely than ever before, and she was filled with a peace and contentment she had not felt since her arrival at Combe House.

She continued slowly on, so absorbed in thought that she almost collided with a man coming down.

"Why, it's Mrs. Summerford! How are you?"

Lucie smiled into Simon Hardy's face. "Hullo, Mr. Hardy, I haven't seen you for ages."

"I can say the same of you – whenever I've called to see Julian it's been too early for you to be up. How is he today, by the way?"

"Fine, thanks. He's beginning to find the cast a nuisance, but we're hoping he won't have to wear it much longer."

"Good. It must be trying for you to have him laid up so long." This was the first time anyone had thought of it from her point of view and Lucie's heart warmed towards him as he fell into step beside her. "If you're on your way to Mayfields I'll walk back a bit of the way with you."

"Oh, do! I didn't expect to see you up here. Have you just come from seeing Ann?"

"No, I live over there." He pointed to a red brick house in the distance.

"What a sweet little place! But I thought you lived on the estate?"

"This *is* part of the estate. The land on either side of us belongs to Combe House."

"I had no idea the property was so large."

"When you get as far as this you're almost on the boundary

of it. It lies right along the top of the hill above the village and seems far more spread out when you come down through Shalford and up again. Mayfields is only just beyond the estate. Were you going there?"

"Yes. I hope Ann's in. I didn't bother to ring up and tell her I was coming, and I must say I'd like a cup of tea before I trek back."

"It's a long way for you to walk," he agreed. "Wouldn't it have been better for you to come by car?"

"I can't drive, and it seemed extravagant to take a taxi."

"I'm sure Ann'll be in. I came down past the back of Mayfields a little while ago and saw her in the garden."

"How is she?"

"I don't know. I didn't stop to speak to her. I'm afraid she hasn't much time for me."

"Oh, I'm sure you're wrong!"

"Thanks for being tactful, but you're too quick not to have noticed her attitude to me."

"That's just her manner, Mr. Hardy! I'm sure she doesn't mean it."

He looked down at her searchingly. "Funny you should stick up for her when you hardly know her. She doesn't usually affect people like that."

"I think she's very unhappy."

"I know she is!"

There was such intensity in his tone that Lucie glanced at him in surprise. But at that moment they breasted the hill and saw Mayfields lying below them.

Simon Hardy halted. "I won't go any further if you don't mind."

"Won't you come in for a cup of tea?"

"I wouldn't dare to intrude on two women wanting a gossip! Thanks all the same." With a wave of his hand he started back down the hill. Then on an afterthought he turned round again. "I'm glad you defended Ann, Mrs. Summerford."

Lucie had no chance to ponder his remark because her sister-in-law came up the path to meet her.

"Hullo there! Nice to see you. I was just having a fit of the blues and hadn't a hope of anyone dropping in to cheer me up."

"I'm glad I've come, then. I wasn't sure you'd be in."

"My dear, I'm always in! Where else could I be, living out here?" Ann opened the front door. "We may as well go straight through to the garden and I'll bring tea out. We've no terrace, I'm afraid – just a rather wild little garden, but it has the merit of not being overplanned like Combe House."

Lucie stepped out on to the long, narrow lawn and paused to admire the clumps of aubrietia which fanned out along its borders. Although there was no other house for miles, a low green hedge separated the garden from the fields and at the bottom of the lawn a gate gave access to a belt of trees.

Ann pushed forward a deck chair. "Make yourself comfortable, I won't be long."

True to her word she returned a few minutes later with the tea tray. "I expect you're dying for a cup after all that walking!"

"I am, rather. By the way, where are the children?"

"Francis has taken them into Teincombe."

"What a pity I've missed them. I always enjoy listening to the way they talk to each other – like a couple of little old men!"

"Never mind, we can have a good natter while they're gone, noisy devils." Ann poured the tea. "What's life been like at the house since Julian's accident?"

"Rather strained, I'm afraid," Lucie said ruefully. "I put my foot in it by insisting on taking up Julian's trays instead of letting his mother do it."

"Incurring maternal wrath, eh? For a little thing you hold your own surprisingly well."

"Not such a little thing at the moment."

"Never mind, it'll soon be over." Ann grinned sympathetically. "Are you going to London or will you have the baby here after all?"

"It looks as if I shall have to have it here now, but I don't mind so much if Julian's with me. It wasn't because I didn't like Combe House that I didn't want to have it there, you know."

"I *do* know. Stick with Julian as long as you can and don't let anyone separate you."

To change the subject, Lucie said: "I met Simon Hardy on my way here and he told me you were in."

"How in heaven's name would he know?" Seeing Lucie's

expression Ann shrugged. "Don't mind me, I always talk this way."

"I know, and personally it doesn't worry me. But some people take it to heart. Simon, for instance."

Ann was suddenly still. "Did he say so?"

"Not in so many words, but I think he feels you don't like him."

"I shouldn't think he cares one way or the other."

There was a short silence and Lucie glanced at her covertly. How unhappy the girl looked! But not even her bright make-up and the lines of discontent on either side of her mouth could disguise the natural pleasantness and intelligence of her face.

"What did you do before you got married?" she asked.

"I was secretary to my uncle – Sir John Ranken."

"Julian's boss?"

"Yes. That's how I met Francis – he came to one of the Foreign Office staff parties. I'll never forget the first time I came down here. The old girl was so thankful I wasn't trying to snatch Julian that she almost forgave me for marrying Francis. Almost. It didn't stop her trying to break up our engagement, though – you may have noticed there's no love lost between us."

"Aren't you dramatising it a bit? Heaven knows I don't hold any brief for her, but surely she's not as dangerous as you make out?"

"I hope you never find out for yourself just how dangerous she can be." Ann flicked her cigarette. "I'm glad you came over today, Lucie. I'm going away with the children next week. My parents haven't seen them for over six months."

"Where do they live?"

"In Warwickshire."

"How funny. I thought you were a Londoner."

"I only went to London to work. My father was Parliamentary Secretary to the Foreign Office, so I suppose it was natural for me to gravitate there too."

Idly Lucie stretched out and picked a piece of grass. "I didn't know you were ever a career girl. Somehow I can't imagine you as one of the world's workers."

"Why on earth not?"

"Oh, I don't mean from the personal point of view, but you

didn't *have* to work for a living like I did, did you?"

"What's that got to do with it?"

"I thought perhaps that was one of the reasons Mrs. Summerford dislikes me."

Ann snorted. "The fact that you worked for a living has nothing to do with it. The old girl would have disliked Queen Elizabeth herself if she'd married one of her sons."

"That's a relief anyway, I couldn't bear snobbery *and* dislike." Lucie glanced down at her watch. "Heavens, it's nearly half past five. I'd better be getting home."

"What's the hurry? Stay for supper and let Francis run you back."

"It's awfully sweet of you, but I must go. Julian's expecting me."

"In that case I'll walk with you to the top of the hill. It's a long way to go on your own."

"I didn't notice it coming, but that was probably because of Simon."

Ann stood up. "Did he walk all the way with you?"

"Only to the top of the hill."

"Scared to come in in case I bit his head off, I suppose?"

"Oh, please don't tell him I mentioned it."

"Of course not, silly – if I did, he might expect me to mend my ways! Come on, I'll get your coat."

Writing letters in Julian's room later that evening Lucie felt a sudden longing to be in London amongst her friends. Most of all she wondered what Piers was doing; whether his ballet had been accepted at last and whether it would be a success. Since leaving the company she had heard nothing from him, although she could hardly expect to after his anger at her desertion.

"Who are you writing to, darling?" Julian asked.

She glanced across the darkening room. How boyish he looked in his gaudy striped pyjamas. Totally unlike the debonair young man she had met at Mimi Delfont's party.

"Some of the company," she replied. "They must be wondering what's happened to me."

"Do you miss them very much?"

"In a way."

"Poor pet, I took you completely out of your environment,

didn't I?" He held out his hand. "Come and sit near me, Lucie love. It's such a long time since I held you in my arms."

She went over and rested her cheek against his, her hair splaying out over the pillow as he stroked it. "Poor Lucie. It's damned miserable for you being cooped up like this, looking after me when I ought to be looking after you."

She kissed his chin, wishing that he and not Simon Hardy had been the first to voice this thought. "I'd be more miserable if I didn't have you to look after."

"Still, it hasn't been much fun for you – married six months and I go and crock myself up like this. It'd be bad enough without the baby, but that must make it even worse."

"Why do you say that? Has your mother said anything to you?"

He looked annoyed. "Why must you always bring Mother into everything?"

"*Me* bring your mother into everything!" She got off the bed. "Ever since we've been here all I've heard from you is Mother, Mother, Mother, and now you accuse *me* of bringing her in!"

"All right, darling, there's no need for you to fly off the handle! It isn't good for you to get excited. Remember your condition."

This was the last straw. "Sometimes I wish to heaven I could forget it!" she cried, and flounced out of the room.

The moment she reached her bedroom Lucie was ashamed of having flared up at such little provocation. Yet it might not do Julian any harm to know what she was thinking. Sometimes it was better to clear the air, even at the expense of a scene, than to leave too many things to rankle. But she could not bear to remain at loggerheads with him for long, and on her way down to dinner went in to make her peace.

"I'm sorry I lost my temper, Julian. It was silly of me."

She looked so forlorn as she stood at the foot of the bed that his face softened. "Come here, little love."

She flew into the curve of his arm and he held her close, feeling her heart beat wildly against his side.

"Don't be annoyed with me, Lucie – I hate it when we quarrel. I love you, darling – never forget that, whatever happens."

She looked into his face. "Whatever happens, I never will."

CHAPTER IV

For the next few weeks Lucie and Julian were happier together. For the first time he began to talk about the baby with interest and a naïve curiosity, laughing at her longing to be slim again, and ridiculing her fears that she would never regain her figure.

Coming down to tea one afternoon Lucie found a letter from Piers on the hall table and opened it instantly, eager for news of the company. His writing had the same flowing vehemence as his speech, and she revelled in the terse wit with which he described the activities of the people she had once known so well. It was not until the last few lines that he told her his ballet had been accepted and he was coming down to Devon to commission an artist to design the décor. At the same time he would like to come along to Combe House and would arrive for lunch unless he heard to the contrary.

Lucie hardly knew which news was the most exciting – that Dennison had taken the ballet or that Piers was coming to lunch. How wonderful to see him again! There were so many questions she wanted to ask – whether Adana had agreed to dance the lead, if Jack Dennison was still as surly first thing in the morning, whether Madame Molina shouted as loudly at the unfortunate corps de ballet – so many questions that she could scarcely wait to see him.

Julian was delighted at his wife's enthusiasm. As his mother had pointed out, Lucie seemed to have become introspective during her pregnancy, and he wondered whether she realised how much he wanted to be up and about again and able to share the little intimacies he had grown to love – watching the way she brushed her hair for a hundred strokes with such determination each night; how she always made her bath too hot and delicately tested it with her toe, a little hissing exclamation escaping her lips; the gentle sound of her breathing when she slept and the suddenness with which she awoke – fast asleep one moment, wide awake the next. It distressed him to see her irritable and tense, and he hoped Piers' visit would shake her out of her depression and give her something different to think about.

To his surprise his mother showed complete lack of enthusiasm at the prospect of Lucie's guest, and when they were alone one morning he reproached her with it.

"I don't know what you mean, dear," she protested. "I'm only too pleased to entertain Lucie's friend. It's just that I'm a little afraid, that's all."

"Afraid of what?"

"I'd rather not say. I don't want to be accused of making mischief."

"Nonsense, Mother. Now you've said so much you might as well finish." He waited. "Well?"

"It's just that I think Lucie might become unsettled if she's reminded of the past."

Unconsciously Julian rubbed the cast on his shoulder. "I think you're worrying unduly, Mother. Lucie's perfectly content now that she has the baby to look forward to."

"I don't agree. I've always felt that if a woman gives up a career to have a baby she always feels the child has come between her and her work."

"But Lucie gave up the ballet before the baby was even thought of."

"That may be, but there's nothing so final as having a child, and subconsciously she probably feels you've trapped her."

"What an awful thing to say!"

The wide mouth tightened. "I'm sorry you think so, Julian, but you did ask for my opinion. In future I shall keep it to myself."

"Don't be silly, Mother. It was just that the idea of trapping Lucie startled me."

"New ideas are often startling."

"I suppose so." He moved uneasily. "Has Lucie ever said anything to you about it?"

"Nothing specific, but I've an instinctive perception where another woman is concerned, and I think her eagerness to get back to London is because she wants to be in the swim of things again – to keep up with her friends, and perhaps her career."

"She wouldn't be able to do that now," he protested.

"Precisely. Which proves my theory that she feels trapped."

She got up and touched his arm. "Now, darling, have a little rest and don't brood over what we've been talking about, or I won't forgive myself for telling you."

But Julian could not get their conversation out of his mind. Did Lucie really feel trapped? Was she hankering to return to London because she wanted to be with him or because she wanted to get back to the ballet? The more he thought about it the more difficult it was to ridicule his mother's arguments and although he longed to ask Lucie point-blank, he was afraid her innate honesty would make her confirm his fears.

Lucie herself had no idea that Julian was looking on Piers' visit as a test, and did nothing to disguise her pleasure at the thought of seeing him. If she wondered at Julian's increasing bouts of irritation she put it down to the tedium of his convalescence, and hoped that when he was allowed to get up he would revert to his usual good humour.

To Lucie's delight Julian was allowed to get out of bed the day of Piers' visit, and came downstairs looking self-consciously handsome in his maroon dressing-gown, the edge of the plaster cast barely visible between its lapels.

They were chatting desultorily in the drawing-room when a car door banged outside, and she hurried from the room to open the front door.

"Piers, how lovely to see you!"

The dancer came slowly up the steps, his quizzical eyes taking in her appearance. "Well, well," he said softly, "so my visit has been for nothing after all!"

"What an uncomplimentary thing to say!"

He linked his arm in hers. "Not at all. I was hoping to persuade you to dance in my ballet."

"But surely it's settled already?"

"Unfortunately not. Adana and I don't see eye-to-eye about interpretation and I was hoping you'd do it with me instead. Now I suppose I'll *have* to give in to that she-wolf." He squeezed her hand. "Never mind, my loss is your husband's gain, and I hope you're both very happy."

"We are," she said staunchly, and ushered him into the drawing-room.

Mrs. Summerford was at her most regal and greeted Piers with such studied graciousness that he bowed extravagantly over her hand, as if anxious to play the part for which she had obviously cast him.

"Do sit down, Mr. Bellamy. Would you care for some sherry? You must excuse my son not being able to play host, but he's recovering from an accident."

Piers looked at Julian enquiringly. "Not a bad one, I hope?"

"Nothing serious – a couple of broken bones."

"If it were me I'd call that very serious." Piers smiled sympathetically, then turned to Lucie. "Well, my pigeon, how do you like living in the depths of the country after the razzle-dazzle?"

Mrs. Summerford gave her no chance to reply. "I'm afraid poor Lucie's finding it a little difficult to settle down, Mr. Bellamy. I dare say you'd find it hard to give up your work too?"

Piers accepted his glass. "The question would never arise, dear lady. With me the ballet comes first – once a dancer, always a dancer."

"How interesting you should say that. It's what I've always thought, but Lucie doesn't agree with me."

"That's because she's in love."

"Are you in this part of the world for long?" Julian put in.

"No, I've done what I came down for. Christian Bernard has agreed to do the décor, Lucie."

"How wonderful!" Her face lit up. "He's the best designer you could have got for it."

"I'm so ignorant of these things," Mrs. Summerford confided. "Forgive my asking, but who is the foreign gentleman you've just mentioned?"

Piers' slanting eyebrows shot up at an even more acute angle. "Christian Bernard is the most brilliant scenic artist of his generation, Mrs. Summerford, and he's no more foreign than we are – he was born in Balham."

"Really? Have you ever heard of him, Julian?"

"Yes, of course," Julian replied shortly. "My mother has spent most of her life in the country, Mr. Bellamy – she knows little or nothing about the arts."

"How silly of me." Piers threw his hostess a charming smile. "Because it's important to me I make the mistake of thinking the ballet is important to everyone."

"I quite understand," she replied graciously. "When something is your entire life it's hard to believe other people are not interested in it."

Piers' eyes darkened, but he recovered instantly. "True, dear lady, but then I could never bear to live in an inartistic atmosphere."

"Would you like another sherry, Piers?" Lucie said quickly.

"Please. A slightly drier one if you have it."

Mrs. Summerford bridled. "I'm afraid that's the driest I have, Mr. Bellamy."

"Ça ne fait rien," he said arily. "It was quite pleasant."

He accepted his second glass with such a show of affectation that Lucie longed to slap him and wondered crossly why he was behaving so badly. Yet he could not be expected to know that he was playing right into her mother-in-law's hands or that the woman would make capital out of it when he had gone. With an effort she tried to break up the conversation.

"We'll go in for lunch as soon as you've finished your drink, Piers."

Her mother-in-law regarded her reprovingly. "Let your friend have his sherry in peace, dear. Gladys will tell me when luncheon is served." She smiled at Piers. "You must forgive Lucie, but she's been so looking forward to your visit that she's over-excited."

"There's nothing to forgive, Mrs. Summerford, and in any case you're flattering me. It wasn't me she's been looking forward to so much as seeing anyone connected with the ballet."

"How clever of you to realise that, Mr. Bellamy – Lucie would never admit such a thing. I'm afraid she's often cross with me for suggesting she misses her work."

"Of course she misses it," Piers agreed. "When you've been doing something for the best part of your life you can't just cut it out like that." He snapped his fingers graphically and Lucie clenched her hands in her lap. The conversation was becoming impossible. She had been acutely uncomfortable while Piers and her mother-in-law had been subtly insulting each other; now that they were agreeing it was even worse. From the scowl on Julian's face it was obvious he had not missed any of the points his mother had been at such pains to make, and she determined to have a word with Piers on their way into the dining-room.

But as if sensing her intention, Mrs. Summerford herself led Piers across the hall, leaving Lucie to help Julian, who scarcely addressed a word to her as they made slow progress behind.

During luncheon Piers monopolised the conversation, led on by his hostess to talk about his work.

"It must be very interesting," Mrs. Summerford conceded over dessert, "and quite difficult to become a dancer at all, from what you've been telling me. Personally, though, it isn't a form of art that's ever appealed to me. It strikes me as too limited."

"That's because you know nothing about it, if you don't mind my saying so."

"I'm not an artistic person, if that's what you mean, but I should have thought music or painting far more expressive."

"Again that's a matter of opinion," Piers said smoothly. "Ask a hundred people what form of art gives them most pleasure and you can get a hundred different answers. Those who like painting will put forward a Rembrandt or Picasso as the highest form of artistic expression; lovers of music will rate a Brahms or Beethoven symphony more moving than anything else in the world. Personally speaking I find the ballet doubly satisfying, for it embraces both art and music."

"To the dancer perhaps, but surely not to the public?"

"You wouldn't say that if you went to Covent Garden and heard the applause," Lucie interrupted. "Ballet doesn't appeal to you, Mother, so you can't see why anybody likes it, but as far as I'm concerned it's the only satisfying form of self-expression."

Mrs. Summerford folded her napkin. "My home and children have always been self-expression enough for me."

Lucie flushed. "I'm sure my husband and child will satisfy me too. My dancing took second place when it came to getting married, because it didn't mean more to me than Julian."

"What do you say to that, Mr. Bellamy?" Mrs. Summerford asked.

"Madam, I marvel that any artist could give up her work and not regret it."

Mrs. Summerford looked triumphant. "You see? Your friend agrees with what I've always said. If I'd worked as hard as you, my dear, I wouldn't have given it up."

"If you'd had the reason I had, it wouldn't have been difficult."

"I hope you appreciate how lucky you were, Julian," his mother said. "You must always try to be worthy of Lucie's sacrifice and make up to her for it."

Julian reddened. "Really, Mother, I wouldn't call Lucie's marriage to me a sacrifice."

"Your mother didn't mean that, darling." Lucie was conscious of the irony of coming to Mrs. Summerford's defence. "She's only suggesting that I miss the ballet more than I do."

Julian lapsed into angry silence and Piers looked from one to the other.

"I'm afraid I don't know what all the argument is about. Ballet is finished for Lucie. I came here hoping to persuade her to dance in my new work, but the minute I saw her I knew it was out of the question. She was so suitable for the part and worked so hard on it with me that it's a great pity, but there it is . . ." He lifted his hands in a gesture of humorous resignation. "We can do nothing except regret the loss of a future ballerina."

Mrs. Summerford regarded him intently. "I thought Lucie was only in the chorus?"

"Don't confuse the chorus of a musical comedy with a corps de ballet, dear lady." Piers was shocked. "Every ballet dancer is a potential star, and Lucie was already beginning to dance solo parts before she left."

"That makes it all the *more* difficult to understand how she could bear to give it up. But let's continue this interesting discussion in the drawing-room, shall we?"

"I'm afraid you'll have to excuse me," Julian put in. "I'm feeling tired and think I'll go back to bed. It's my first time up today," he explained to Piers, "and I don't want to overdo it."

The dancer smiled. "Of course not. You can leave the ladies safely in my hands."

"Thank you, I'm sure I can." And brusquely refusing Lucie's offer of help, Julian hobbled out of the room.

Julian no longer being present, Mrs. Summerford subsided into her usual hauteur and made no effort to entertain Piers. "The dancer is your friend" her attitude seemed to suggest, and left Lucie to do all the talking, an attitude that Lucie found difficult in her mother-in-law's presence.

Immediately coffee was finished Piers stood up to go.

"There's such a lot to do now that you can't dance the part. And in any case I want to have a talk with Dennison tonight." With a flourish he kissed Mrs. Summerford's hand. "It's been so nice meeting you. I hope I shall have the pleasure of seeing you at the theatre one evening."

They moved out into the hall and Piers kissed Lucie on both cheeks. "Don't keep yourself so strange in future. Get in touch with us when you come back to London and don't forget to let me know if you have a little Nureyev or a Fonteyn!"

Strangely enough Piers' visit put Mrs. Summerford in a good humour, and for the next few days she talked about him in such glowing terms that it was almost as if she were trying to make her son jealous. At first Lucie could scarcely credit this, then decided ironically that it might not do Julian any harm, unaware that in his secret state of conflict it was the worst possible emotion for him to feel. She did not know how much he longed to hear her tell him she did not regret giving up the ballet, or that she would have made the same decision again if she had to. Indeed, she avoided the subject so pointedly that Julian began to feel his mother had been right when she said Lucie missed the ballet too much to talk about it.

A fortnight after Piers' visit the cast was removed from Julian's shoulder and apart from a bandage around his ankle he was almost normal again. Now that he was up and about Lucie expected him to return to their room, but he stayed on in the sick-room and for several days she was afraid to ask him why. But one afternoon her reticence seemed so false that she decided to speak to him while her mother-in-law was still resting. Julian was her husband, her lover, the father of her child, and such false modesty was unnatural between them.

She found him sitting on the terrace with his feet up and went over and kissed the top of his head. "Hullo, darling. Had a nice doze?"

"On and off," he smiled. "Didn't sleep much last night and I was hoping to make up for it this afternoon. One can't do it to order, though."

Lucie sat down in a deck chair. "I didn't sleep well either, but that's because I miss you."

"I'm here, silly!"

"I know, darling, but having you down the corridor isn't the same as turning my head and being able to see you. When are you going to come back to our room? There's no need for you to stay in the sick-room any longer."

"Wouldn't you rather be on your own until it's over?"

"What makes you say that?"

"No particular reason, darling," he said awkwardly, "it's just that I want to do whatever's best for you. Don't you think it'd be better if I stayed where I am for the time being?"

"If I did I wouldn't have asked you to come back. But if that's the way you feel perhaps it'd be better if you stayed where you are." She stood up and with a rustle of skirts was gone.

Julian picked up his book, but the memory of her face came between him and the words and he put it aside and stared reflectively across the lawn. Women were unpredictable, heaven knew, but surely his mother was right when she said that someone as sensitive as Lucie would prefer to be alone at the moment, even though she might feel it her duty to ask him to return?

With a sigh he bent his head to the print and when he had concentrated sternly for a few minutes was soon absorbed again.

Julian's refusal to return to their bedroom hurt Lucie so much that she could no longer talk to him naturally. She remained in her room for long periods, only coming down for meals when Francis and her mother-in-law were sure to be there, and went for long, slow walks by herself, occasionally meeting Simon Hardy, who would accompany her part of the way and show her different areas of the estate. His wholesome sanity and kindliness was unchanged and she grew to look on him as the one person to whom she could turn for companionship.

Ann was still away and Lucie missed her sister-in-law's friendly bluntness, wondering what she would have said to the latest developments at Combe House. From Piers there was no word, but she was not surprised at his silence knowing how busy he must be, and three weeks later read in the evening papers that the Dennison company's new ballet had been performed with great success. In Piers Bellamy, one critic declared, England had a choreographer of outstanding merit, a young artist who would add immeasurably to the prestige of British ballet. There were photographs of Piers and Adana in the costumes of the pas de deux and below them a paragraph stating that the company had been invited to America, and would accept as soon as their season in London was over.

Sitting in the drawing-room just before dinner Lucie looked up excitedly from the newspaper on her knees. "Oh, Julian, isn't it wonderful – at last Piers is beginning to have the success he's always dreamed of!"

"He didn't strike me as a dreamer," her husband said drily. "I thought him a very practical man."

"What a silly thing to say! Of course he's practical – he has to be. But he must be a dreamer as well, or he wouldn't have any ideas to express. I'm glad they're going to America – it's something he's wanted Jack Dennison to do for ages."

"Why?" her mother-in-law asked.

"Because he's always wanted to make a ballet film, and he thinks that if he's seen by the Americans he'll have a better chance of going to Hollywood."

"So he's got an eye for filthy lucre too?" Julian said sarcastically.

"It isn't the money," Lucie expostulated, "but the fact that he'll reach such a large audience. Anyway, do be consistent, Julian. First you accuse him of being a dreamer and then find fault when he's practical! He's just as entitled to make money as anyone else, and he works much harder for what he earns than most people."

"There's no need for you to defend him. I'm sure he can look after himself. Anyone as rude as he is doesn't need a champion."

"In what way was he rude?"

"I'd hardly call the way he criticized the sherry a mark of good manners!"

Lucie flushed. "I wouldn't call some of your mother's remarks to him good manners, either!"

"Damn it, Lucie," Julian said angrily, "leave Mother out of this!"

"Children! children!" Mrs. Summerford entreated. "Julian, you mustn't lose your temper with Lucie just because she's proud of Mr. Bellamy."

"Why the hell *should* she be proud of him? He's nothing to do with her!"

"I'm proud of him because he's my friend and I admire his work!" Lucie burst out. "He's got a wonderful future and one day I'll be even prouder to have known him and worked with him than I am already. Now if you'll excuse me, I'm going to my room."

The door shut sharply behind her and there was an uncomfortable silence. Then Julian buried his head in his hands.

"I don't know what's been the matter with me the last few months. I'm rude to you, bad-tempered with Lucie and a misery to myself."

"Darling boy, don't take it to heart!" Mrs. Summerford went to his side. "You're still on edge from your accident and Lucie doesn't know you well enough to leave you alone when you're like this. Don't forget you didn't know each other very long when you were married." She put her hand on his head. "Oh, Julian, why didn't you wait a little longer? Lucie's a sweet girl, but she's not the right wife for you. There's so much more to marriage than a passing infatuation. You've got to share the same outlook and values and the same code of morals."

"Fundamentally we do."

"I wish I could be sure of that, Julian. Lucie's a temperamental girl, erratic and impulsive, and you're down-to-earth and analytical. You're so different you're bound to clash. And another thing, dear – try not to show your jealousy of Mr. Bellamy. After all, he's known Lucie much longer than you, and shared a part of her life that's very important to her."

"I didn't think I could ever be jealous of Bellamy, but I suppose I am." He smiled wryly. "You seem to know me better than I know myself!"

"That's not surprising, darling. Now let's have some sherry before dinner, just you and I." She hesitated. "Unless you want to go up and see how Lucie is first?"

He shook his head. "You're very tactful, Mother, but this time I'm going to leave Lucie to come round on her own."

"I suppose you're right. After all, you can't give in to her all the time – she's got to learn to control herself, and the sooner she does the better for your peace of mind."

At dinner nothing was said about the argument and Lucie

left Julian and his mother together in the drawing-room immediately after coffee. Lying wakeful in bed, she waited for him to come in and make the peace, but it was half past eleven before she heard his footsteps on the stairs and he went straight into the sick-room without even hesitating at the end of the corridor. It was the first time the sun had gone down on their anger, and as his door closed she turned her face into the pillow and cried herself to sleep.

The following morning she was heavy-eyed and listless and did not go downstairs until lunch-time when she was surprised to see Mrs. Summerford sitting in solitary state at the dining-room table.

"Ah, good morning, Lucie – feeling better?"

"Yes, thank you." She sat down and accepted her plate.

"Julian asked me to apologise for not being here, but he wanted a breath of fresh air. Francis had to go into Exeter to pick up some farm implements, so he thought he might as well go along for the ride and have lunch there. He left early and didn't want to come in and disturb you."

"That's all right, Mother, you needn't apologise for him."

"I'm not apologising for him. I'm merely giving you his message."

They spoke little after that and immediately the meal was over Lucie stood up and pushed back her chair. "Excuse me, Mother, I'm going for a walk."

"Is it wise, dear? You look rather pale, and I'm sure a rest would do you more good."

"I feel quite all right," Lucie said firmly. "I'll be back for tea."

Slipping on a coat and scarf, she set off down the drive. Although Ann was still away she walked in the direction of Mayfields, and had reached the other side of Shalford when the mist which had been shrouding the hills developed into a steady downpour. She would be drenched before she could reach the village again, and decided to take refuge in Simon's cottage. Half-way down the narrow lane he had pointed out to her on one of their walks she saw an empty barn, and made her way across the fields towards it, her shoes squelching in the mud.

Once inside, she untied her scarf and shook her hair free, hoping the rain would soon abate. But it continued relentlessly and she looked round for somewhere to sit. A ramshackle wheelbarrow was overturned in one corner, and the broken end of a tractor seat was overturned in the other; neither seemed safe enough to take her weight. In the far corner a narrow flight of stairs led up to a half-filled hay-loft and she climbed up and settled herself down with a sigh of relief. It was warm here, the fresh smell pleasant and soothing, and tired from her walk and sleepless night her eyelids grew heavy and she fell asleep.

She awoke with a start to find that the sun was shining again. Scrambling to her feet she began to descend the stairs. Going down was more difficult than coming up, for there was no rail to steady her, and she was nearly at the bottom before she remembered her scarf drying on the hay. She turned to fetch it, and without warning her foot slipped on the wooden step. Desperately she clutched at the ladder, but the rotting wood gave way in her hand and she fell to the ground, one leg twisted beneath her. For several minutes she lay on the floor too dazed to move. Then gingerly she stood up, relieved to find no bones were broken, and limped slowly across the barn to the entrance. On the threshold the first pain came.

It was so violent that she bent double until it had passed and she could walk on. Again it came, this time with increased intensity, and by the time she reached the end of the field she knew she would never be able to get home unaided.

It might have been minutes or hours that she half lay, half knelt on the sodden grass, but suddenly the barking of a dog and a man's voice pentrated the dark reaches of pain, and she looked up to see Simon Hardy.

"Mrs. Summerford, what's the matter?"

"Fell down – barn steps – sheltering from rain." His face quivered and receded. "Please get me home quickly. The baby – I'm terribly afraid!"

A long time later Lucie awoke to find Julian bending over her. For a moment she could not think why his face was haggard and strained. Then memory returned and weak tears filled her eyes.

"Oh, Julian, the baby – what's happened to the baby?"

"A little girl, my darling, a lovely little girl."

Relief flooded through her. "Let me see her."
"Not yet, darling. I'll bring her in when you've had another sleep."
Her eyes flew open in alarm. "Why can't I see her now? I don't believe she's all right – you're not telling me the truth!"
"The baby's perfectly all right, darling, I swear it. But she's such a tiny creature they're keeping her in an oxygen tent for the time being."
Lucie started to cry. "Oh, Julian, how could I have failed her like that? It was terrible – if it hadn't been for Simon I don't know what I'd have done."
"Thank God he found you when he did." Julian's voice was husky. "You might have died, my darling."
"Dancers don't die so easily! We're a tough lot, you know – I'm strong." She smiled feebly and closed her eyes. "I'm a strong little thing." And suddenly she was asleep.
Julian looked down at her for a long time. During the terrible hours of waiting he had castigated himself for allowing Lucie to drift so far apart from him in the past few months. What a fool he had been to let her live through the whole of this experience on her own, when she must have needed him so much. Where had they gone wrong, what had first started the rift – had it been his fault or hers? But the answer eluded him, and with a sigh he tip-toed out of the room.
At the head of the stairs he paused, then turned down the corridor to his mother's room.
Mrs. Summerford was sitting up in bed, a breakfast tray on her knees. "Sorry to eat without you, darling, but after last night I thought a morning in bed would do me good."
"Of course, Mother." He bent and kissed her.
"Would you like to have something up here with me?"
"No, thanks. I'm not hungry."
"Don't be silly, Julian, you must eat. Lucie's perfectly all right now, and there's no need to worry."
"But what about the baby? Do you think she'll be all right?"
"The baby? Of course, the baby. Somehow I can't think of you as a father."
"Well, I was left in no doubt about it last night." His face softened. "Funny little thing, isn't she?"
"Babies are all like that to begin with, and then, of course,

being six weeks premature makes a difference. I wonder what can have caused the accident?"

"Simon said she told him she'd taken shelter in the barn and slipped on the stairs leading to the loft."

"The barn near Mayfields, do you mean? What on earth was she doing there? She knew Ann was away."

"Perhaps she just wanted a direction for her walk, poor darling."

"Perhaps." Mrs. Summerford stirred her coffee. "Although it was rather a long way to go in her condition. She should have been more careful of herself. When I saw Mr. Hardy carrying her in I was afraid she'd injured the child."

"If only I'd been here!"

"I'm glad you weren't." She smiled. "Now don't look so miserable, in a few weeks Lucie will be perfectly all right."

But it was nearly a month before Lucie was allowed downstairs. By this time the family nannie was installed, and whether it was because her mother-inn-law had arranged it, or because the woman was so much older than she had anticipated, Lucie disliked Nurse Richards on sight and made up her mind that as soon as she was well enough she would look after the baby herself.

A few weeks after the birth Julian's sick leave ended and he was only able to get down to Shalford at weekends. He was kindness itself to Lucie, as if trying to atone for everything that had gone before, and she lived through the week looking forward to his homecoming. She had expected him to want the baby christened after his mother, but he raised no objection to calling her Amanda, after her own mother. She was a frail little creature with light hair and grey eyes, and would lie quietly in her cot, only waking to be fed.

Lucie was perfectly well before she told Julian she wanted to return to London.

"I don't think you're strong enough yet, darling," he demurred, "and anyway, it seems a pity to leave the country during the summer. There's not much to be said for living in town during this heat."

They were sunbathing on the lawn, and looking up at the blue sky and the masses of flowers in the beds around them, Lucie had to admit the truth of what he said.

"Even so," she argued, "you might start trying to get us a flat. I definitely want to move in the autumn."

"There's plenty of time to worry about that. Turn over on your back and cook your other side – the sun's beating on your head."

Obediently she rolled over and closed her eyes, but after a moment's silence returned to the attack. "All the same, you'd better keep an eye open, Julian. If you wait until the autumn we may not be able to find anything."

"All right, my love, but it won't be easy. One of the chaps at the office has a service flat in a block near Baker Street – he may know of something. I'll ask him."

"A service flat won't be any good with a baby."

There was a moment's hesitation before he replied. "I didn't know you intended taking Amanda. Don't you think she'd be better off down here?"

Lucie rolled over and sat up. "Good heavens, Julian, I wouldn't dream of leaving her behind!"

"But it seems a shame to subject her to a winter in London when she could stay in the country and build up her strength."

"Nonsense! What about the people who never take their children *out* of London?"

"They've got no choice, darling, but we have. We can easily leave her here with Mother and come down at weekends."

"I wouldn't dream of it," Lucie repeated sharply. "Amanda must be with us."

He yawned and patted her hand. "Well, there's no point in crossing our bridges before we come to them. In any case, I'll probably be posted abroad."

"I'd forgotten that." She leaned over and looked at him. The unhealthy pallor of the months after his accident had gone, and with the sun shining on his closed eyes and his mouth relaxed, he looked so young and untroubled that she doubted if Amanda's advent had had any effect on him whatever.

"Where do you think they'll send you, Julian? I hope it's France or Italy – I've always wanted to go to Rome."

"Don't get excited, baby – I haven't the least idea yet. It may even be Washington."

"How wonderful! I'd love to see what America's really like.

Mandy might even grow up with a Yankee accent if we were there long enough!"

He opened his eyes and pulled her against him. "Wouldn't you rather we were on our own, like we were in Paris? After all, we haven't had much life together since we were married."

Lucie rubbed her cheek on the soft hairs on his chest. "I would in a way, but I don't see how Amanda will spoil it."

"She wouldn't *spoil* it, but I'd much rather have you on my own. You're such a little thing, I can hardly imagine you as a mother at all."

"You don't have to do any imagining, darling, Amanda's proof!"

"Even if you had ten children you'd still be a baby to me." He bit her ear. "You smell so full of sun, I could eat you!"

"Don't treat me too much like a baby, Julian – you may get a shock one day." She kissed the tip of his nose and turned round to face the sun again, wishing he had more paternal feeling for Amanda and less for herself.

Lucie had expected her mother-in-law to be very proprietorial of the baby, but she seemed content to leave everything to the nurse, a tall, big-boned woman with a heavy face and large, red hands. The only time she took any notice of her granddaughter was at weekends when Julian was home, and Lucie got the impression that she was not really fond of the baby at all.

At first the old nurse treated her with a certain amount of respect, but gradually her deference to Mrs. Summerford increased to an exaggerated degree, and as it did so, lessened towards Lucie. Nevertheless, the woman had a peculiar gentleness with the baby and, as she did not intend keeping her for very much longer, Lucie decided to allow things to go on as they were.

Slowly August gave way to September and as the lazy days of summer drew to a close Lucie's determination to leave Combe House strengthened. She and Julian had never discussed their estrangement, but the resentment she bore him for his lack of understanding in the months previous to Amanda's birth had not quite disappeared, and occasionally she experienced a surge of antagonism towards him – an antagonism that made her feel guilty. Not even the renewal of the physical bond could restore their unity, and for the first time she realized that one could be bodily close without mental or emotional understanding.

Ann was already back at Mayfields, but Lucie had only spoken to her on the telephone, and respecting her sister-in-law for not being hypocrite enough to come to the house when Mrs. Summerford was out of the way, she decided to take the baby over to see her instead.

Nurse Richards received her instructions to get Amanda ready with ill-concealed hostility. "Do you think it's wise to take her out of the house yet, madam?"

"I don't see why not." Lucie bent over the cot and Amanda's grey eyes looked up at her unblinkingly. "I'm sure it won't do her any harm, Nurse. It's a lovely day and my sister-in-law hasn't seen her yet."

Every line of the nurse's face registered disapproval. "I don't think it'll do her any good to be shaken up in a taxi."

"I'll carry her in my arms," Lucie said equably. "I'm sure she'll enjoy the ride!"

"If you insist, madam, but I don't think Mrs. Summerford will approve."

"As far as Amanda's concerned, Nurse, *I* am Mrs. Summerford. Kindly remember that."

Lucie turned on her heel and left the room, conscious of having won a victory at the expense of making another enemy at Combe House.

Ann showed unexpected tenderness with Amanda, and watching her coo over the baby Lucie thought how strange it was that such a brusque, sharp-tongued young woman should be so maternal.

"You ought to have a little girl, Ann," she said.

"I've got enough on my hands with the twins."

"But wouldn't you like another baby?"

"The boys have tied me quite enough as it is."

Quickly Lucie changed the subject and for the rest of the afternoon they talked about Ann's holiday in Warwick. At four o'clock Francis brought Simon Hardy in for tea, and Ann's demeanour changed so noticeably that the man apologised for coming.

"Francis can bring you if he likes," Ann shrugged. "One more cup to wash up won't kill me."

He made no reply to this and sat down next to Lucie. "Are you better now?"

"Much better, thank you." Although he had seen her since the birth of the baby, this was the first time she had encountered him without her mother-in-law being present and she was glad to be able to talk more freely. "I never thanked you properly for coming to my rescue, Simon. I don't know what I'd have done if you hadn't."

"I'm glad I was there." He leaned over the carry-cot. "I feel I've quite a proprietorial interest in this young lady."

The sound of his voice awoke Amanda and she started to cry.

"I say," he said admiringly, "what a lusty yell for such a tiddler! Can I pick her up?"

"Do you know how to?"

"Oh, I'm quite an old hand. I've a couple of nephews in Scotland, and bachelor uncles are always in demand." With surprising dexterity he picked Amanda up and she stopped crying and stared into his face with blank fixity. "There's a good little girl, always stop crying for Uncle Simon."

Coming back into the room with the tea-tray, Ann regarded him ironically. "My, my, quite the mother's help! I'll always know who to call on when I'm in trouble!"

"A good idea," he said affably, and sat down with the baby on his knee.

Ann planked the teapot on the table. "You'd better put her down while you have your tea."

"I can manage."

"No, you can't. Here, let me take her." She scooped the baby up in her arms, flushing as their hands met and she moved hastily away.

Lucie found it heartening to be treated as a responsible person instead of the ineffectual creature her mother-in-law always made her feel, and she was glad she had insisted on bringing Amanda to Mayfields. But when she got home she was left in no doubt that the nurse had complained to Mrs. Summerford, for her mother-in-law mentioned it as soon as they sat down to dinner.

"I know you want to be with Amanda as much as possible,

Lucie, but Nurse Richards is in charge of her and she was very upset when you took her out this afternoon."

"I'm sorry about that, Mother, but it didn't do Amanda any harm, and after all, she is my child."

"But don't you think it would have been more tactful to have asked Nurse Richards to go with you?"

"It never crossed my mind. Anyway, I thought she'd have appreciated having the afternoon free. Most nurses would."

"Nurse Richards is rather exceptional, my dear. She's been in our family for many years and it would be as well not to upset her."

"I've never heard of anyone having to placate their nannie, and I don't see why I should."

"You must do as you please, of course, but you're making my position rather difficult. I'm the one she'll come and complain to."

"Why should she?" Lucie said quietly. "I'm Amanda's mother."

Mrs. Summerford poured herself a glass of water. "I hate to mention it, Lucie, but considering I pay Nurse Richards I don't think it's too much to expect a say in what affects her."

"*You* pay her? But I thought Julian . . .?"

"Julian has no money of his own apart from his salary."

"Surely we can manage on that?"

"I doubt it. Lucie, do you know Julian's financial position?"

Lucie hesitated and Mrs. Summerford went on: "I thought not. I'm forgetting you hardly knew one another when you married." She folded her hands on the table. "I'd always hoped Julian would reach a settled position in the Foreign Office before he tied himself down, but young people in love never stop to think about the future. It was lucky for him that I did."

"What do you mean?"

"My son has always spent every penny he earns. I've never wanted him to do otherwise because one day he'll have this house and my money. When you were in Paris he spent most of what he had saved in the past few years."

"But why didn't he tell me the truth – what was the point in pretending?"

"Perhaps he was afraid you married him for his money!"

Lucie's face flamed. "What a horrible thing to say!"

Mrs. Summerford shrugged. "Be that as it may, Julian's income is very small. It was hardly enough for him to live on in London when he was a bachelor, let alone support a wife and child."

Suddenly Lucie understood a great deal that had been incomprehensible before. Now she knew the reason Julian wanted Amanda to remain at Combe House and why, if they went to live in London, it would have to be in a small flat. But why hadn't he told her his true position himself? Did he really believe it would make any difference to her love for him?

"So you see, Lucie," her mother-in-law continued, "it would be expedient to allow Nurse Richards full control. She naturally feels responsible to me and you can't blame her." She smiled. "Now you mustn't worry about what I've told you. Julian is far from a poor man – as I said before, he will inherit most of my money and the income from the estate will be quite sufficient for the upkeep of the house and staff."

"As far as I'm concerned, Mother, Combe House belongs to you. As for Nurse Richards, I can understand now why she's never liked taking orders from me, and in view of what you've just told me I'd like you to let Nurse Richards go."

Mrs. Summerford flushed. "Really, Lucie, how proud you are! You must learn to accept kindnesses more graciously. Surely you know I love doings things for Julian? I'm only too happy to help you both. Please don't say any more about it. Anyway, you're not strong enough to look after Amanda yourself."

"What about all the women who have to look after their children as soon as they come out of hospital?"

"They're not highly strung and emotional like you."

Lucie threw down her table napkin angrily. "Why do you keep trying to make out that I'm unstable? You're always implying it, especially when Julian's here. I assure you I'm perfectly normal."

"I'd hardly call your attitude to me a normal one. Your ingratitude is unbelievable!" Mrs. Summerford stood up and crossed majestically to the door. "Ever since you came to my house you've disliked me and resented my love for Julian – and his for me. I've exercised forbearance in the hope that you'd learn that a man can love his mother just as much as his wife. More so, in fact, because a mother knows and understands her child far better than any stranger."

"How dare you call me a stranger!" Lucie said hotly.

"I cannot think of you as anything else. And I certainly wouldn't compare the love of a few months to the love I've borne Julian for thirty years."

"I should think not. I hope my love for Julian will never become as selfish and possessive as yours!"

"And I hope no daughter-in-law will ever talk to you as you've been talking to me. I don't like you, Lucie, but I wouldn't even wish that on you."

The door closed behind her and Lucie was left alone in the room, angry and confused.

CHAPTER V

No matter how carefully Lucie analysed the quarrel she remained convinced that Mrs. Summerford wanted to part her from Julian, and that she was up against an extremely clever and subtle woman who would stop at nothing.

Now she knew that Julian was not paying Nurse Richards she spent as little time as possible in the nursery, consoling herself with the thought that it would not be long before they moved to London and she could have her baby completely to herself.

Friday dragged interminably. Julian never arrived home until the evening, and when Ann telephoned and asked her to go for a walk in the afternoon she accepted gladly. Mrs. Summerford watched her get ready in acid silence, but Lucie was past caring, and set off to meet Ann in Shalford, unaware that as she walked down into the village Julian's car drew up at Combe House and he hurried into the hall, calling her name.

"Is that you, Julian?" His mother appeared in the drawing-room door. "I didn't expect you so soon."

"Managed to get off earlier than usual. I've got some news. Where's Lucie?"

"Out with Ann. But never mind, come and tell me instead."

They went into the drawing-room and Julian sat down on the sofa, his eyes bright with excitement.

"Well?" she said, "I'm waiting."

"I've been appointed Attaché to the Swedish Legation and Sir John's dropped the hint that if I'm any good I'll be off to Washington within a year."

"Oh, Julian, that's wonderful! I always knew you'd be successful."

He grinned. "You talk as if I'd been made an Ambassador at the very least! Still, it's a step in the right direction and it'll give me an increase in pay. Lucie and I will be able to have a decent little flat in town now."

"You know very well I've always offered to give you whatever you need."

"I know you have, but I've accepted too much from you already. As it is I'll never be able to repay you for all you've done for us since our marriage." He frowned and looked at his watch. "I wish Lucie were here – I've been looking forward all day to telling her my news. Does she see much of Ann?"

"Yes, and I'm not very happy about it, either. As you know, Ann's never liked me and she's prejudicing Lucie against me."

Julian looked disconcerted. "Are you sure?"

"Positive. Let's not beat about the bush, Julian. Lucie doesn't like me and it's silly to pretend she does." She stood up and moved to the window, a tall, solid figure in keeping with the gracious proportions of the room. "I'm not a young woman, Julian, and I haven't had a very easy life. Your father was constantly abroad when you and Francis were little and the responsibility for your upbringing and education rested completely on me. I'd always hoped that when my sons married I would gain two daughters, but both Lucie and Ann have resented me and gone out of their way to show me I'm not needed. I'm sorry for Lucie – if I wasn't I'd have asked you to take her away before now; as it is I don't think I can go on much longer."

Julian ran a hand through his hair.

"I don't know what to say. I know Lucie hasn't been too happy here, but I was hoping it would work itself out."

"Well, it hasn't. Why, only this week we had an argument because I told her she wasn't strong enough to look after the baby."

"What nonsense! Of course she isn't strong enough. Anyway, Nurse Richards is perfectly adequate, isn't she?"

"I've always thought so. But I'm afraid Lucie resents the fact that Nurse comes to me for orders. I can see her point of view perfectly – don't think I can't – but after all Nurse has known me for many years and automatically turns to me for advice."

"The whole thing is childish and unnecessary," Julian said impatiently. "I'll have a word with Lucie over the weekend."

"I wish you would. I'm no longer young enough to pass over constant bickering. And while we're having this little discussion, I've a confession to make which I don't think you're going to like." She hesitated, so obviously looking for words that he prompted her.

"Come on, old lady, out with it."

"Oh, Julian, it's rather difficult. You see – I – well, when Lucie and I were arguing the other day I lost my temper – something I haven't done for years – and said that if she wanted to live in London you wouldn't be able to do so on your present income."

Julian stiffened imperceptibly. "I'm sorry you told her that. It was something I'd rather have done myself."

"I know, dear, but I'd no idea you hadn't. It was only when I saw her amazement that I realized she didn't know your position at all."

"Lucie hasn't any business sense, Mother, and I've never discussed money with her at all. However, the question doesn't arise now. I can afford to take a decent sized flat and have her and Amanda in town with me."

Mrs. Summerford looked at him earnestly. "Do you really think that's wise? I don't want to interfere, but you know yourself how highly-strung Lucie is. Do you think she's fit to take on the responsibility of a baby?"

"Don't you?"

"Quite frankly, no." She leaned forward. "Look at the illogical way she's behaved since she's been here; her excitability and lack of self-control; the way she argues and loses her temper! And then this mania for long walks on her own, even in the last months of her pregnancy. Of course, I knew she was brooding about missing her chance in Mr. Bellamy's new ballet, but even so her behaviour was strange. Very, very strange."

"Why are you taking that tone? What are you trying to say?"

"Nothing, Julian. I've already said too much."

"Please," he said quietly, "you've already gone too far to stop now."

"Very well." She took a deep breath. "I've always thought it – odd – that Lucie should have had her accident immediately she heard about the success of the new ballet."

Julian's face lost all its colour. "Do you mean . . .?"

"That Mr. Bellamy wanted Lucie to go back to the company and Amanda was in the way."

The silence was final. Then Julian moved over to the table and stubbed out his cigarette. "If you'll excuse me, Mother, I'll go up and see the baby."

When Ann said good-bye to Lucie later that afternoon she swung quickly down the hill, and as ever when she was alone her thoughts flew to Simon. How much longer would she be able to keep up a pretence of hostility when her every instinct was to fly into his arms? What would he do if she begged him to rescue her from a marriage that was slowly sapping her humour, her intelligence and her self-respect? Since Lucie had told her he was hurt by her continual unfriendliness, she had hugged to herself the joy of knowing that he minded what her attitude was! If only Francis wouldn't try to make them friends.

Francis! Her mouth drew down into a line of contempt. It was hard to believe that the love she had felt for him could have died such an ignominious death. She thought back over the six years of their marriage, remembering her incredulous shock when she had discovered that she took second place in his life. For the hundredth time she wondered how she could have married him without seeing the fundamental weakness in his nature; how she, who had wanted a man to be proud of, had chosen a weakling with an obsession for his mother.

If only she had had the courage to insist on their leaving Combe House earlier, how different their story might have been! But by the time they had moved it was already too late; her love had wilted under her contempt and she no longer cared what Francis thought or felt.

If it weren't for the children ... Ann's face softened as she thought how much they had changed for the better since they had come to Mayfields. At Combe House they had been Mrs. Summerford's youngest sons, submissive and pathetically eager to make the old woman like them; away from her autocratic domination they were developing into natural, lovable little boys who gave their mother the love they had once anxiously lavished on their grandmother.

She reached the end of the field, clambered over the stile and walked through the shadowy woods towards the back of the house, so intent on her thoughts that she did not notice the man approaching until she was almost upon him. Simon!

"Hullo, Ann."

For a long moment she stared at him as if he were a figment of her imagination – as if the intensity of her longing had conjured him up before her.

It was the first time Simon had seen her with neither boredom nor irritation on her face, and he scarcely knew her for the same woman.

"I didn't know you came along here," he said lamely.

Instantly the irritation was back. "Why shouldn't I? It isn't your right of way."

"I only meant that you usually go home by the road."

"How the hell do you know? Do you watch me?"

"It's easy to see a solitary figure on the hill."

"Meaning that I'm conspicuous, I suppose?"

She made to move past, but suddenly he barred her way, his face strangely set and his voice when he spoke so low that it was almost a whisper.

"Don't talk to me like that, Ann – for God's sake don't wreak your hurt on me!"

"What do you mean?"

"Don't you know I'd give everything I possess for one nice word from you?"

She drew back, startled. "I'm sorry – I didn't think. If I seem unfriendly –"

"I want more than friendship!" he burst out. "I want to take you in my arms and make you forget everything that hurts you. Oh, Ann, I can't bear to see you so unhappy. I love you so much!" He stopped and ran a hand across his eyes. "Forgive me, I don't know what I'm saying . . . I must be mad – I've no right."

"Simon, don't take it back! For God's sake don't take it back!"

There was an agony of joy in her voice and without another word, with complete unison of movement, they were in each other's arms, clinging together as if their desire could surmount all the barriers that lay between them.

Away at Combe House Lucie was in Julian's arms, determined to make him agree to take her away. "Darling Julian, I've missed you so," she whispered. "I can't bear to be parted from you much longer! Take me to London with you, Julian. I don't mind where we live as long as we're together."

"There's something I want to tell you first." He moved to the window-seat and she sat down by his side and rested her head on his shoulder. But although he put his arm around her there was no warmth in the caress. "I got back earlier today because I've some news for you," he began. "I've been appointed attaché to the Swedish Legation and will be in London until the middle of next year at the very least."

"Darling, that's wonderful! Now we can have a home of our own!"

"It isn't as simple as that."

"You needn't explain," she said quickly. "Your mother told me you haven't any money apart from your salary. But I don't mind living economically as long as we're together."

"There won't be any necessity for economy – the upgrade in income is quite sufficient for us to manage on."

"That's the best news I've heard for a long time!"

"Does money mean so much to you, then?"

Something in his voice frightened her. "Why do you say that? Your mother asked me the same thing today. Have you been talking to her?"

"What if I have?"

"You've no right to," she said sharply. "Don't you know better than to discuss your wife with your mother? Haven't you any loyalty to me, Julian?"

"There's no need to get excited, Lucie, you'll only lose your temper."

"Get excited!" she cried. "That's what I've been trying not to do ever since I set foot in this house. I've continually had to curb my temper and disgust!"

"Disgust is hardly the right word to use where Mother's concerned!"

"My position isn't right where your mother's concerned! You wouldn't have implied what you did if you hadn't been talking to her! Oh, Julian, what's happened to us? Don't you know that your love and our baby are the most important things in my life?" Tears poured down her cheeks, but she dashed them away. "Can't you see where we're heading – can't you face up to things before we go the same way as Francis and Ann?"

"I might have known Ann had something to do with this!" he burst out. "I should have realised all this vituperation didn't come from you! You're too easily led by Ann's hatred of Mother."

"I'm not! I've got eyes in my head and I can see things for myself. Ann's tried her best, but she –"

"For God's sake don't let's quarrel about Ann and Francis! We've enough to contend with already." He made an effort to control his temper. "Sit down again, Lucie, and listen to me."

She gestured hopelessly and did as she was told.

"When I first suggested you stay down here with Amanda you almost bit my head off. Now there's no financial need for it I suppose you'll resent it even more, but I still think you ought to stay. No, Lucie, let me finish. It isn't that I don't want you in town – heaven knows I miss you as much as you miss me – I only think it would be better for you to stay in the country until you're strong again. After all, the baby's only a few months old and you don't want to be parted from her, do you?"

"There's no reason why I should be."

"I think there is," he said steadily. "A few more months of peace and quiet –"

"Peace and quiet!" Lucie spoke between clenched teeth. "Am I an invalid or a lunatic, that I should need all this peace and quiet? I'm a healthy young woman, Julian, and it's peace and quiet that's driving me mad! I grant you I'm temperamental, but I'm an artist –"

"You *were* an artist."

"I haven't changed my temperament because I married you!"

"Perhaps you regret it!"

"What do you mean?"

"It's obvious you miss your dancing more than you've admitted. Isn't that why you want to get back to London? Perhaps you think that once we're there you'll be able to persuade me to let you return to the ballet?"

"If that was the reason I wanted to return to London I wouldn't wait for your permission. Wives aren't their husbands' chattels any more, you know." She tossed back her hair angrily. "But why have you brought all this up now? Why should you accuse me of wanting to go back to the ballet?"

"Because ever since your dancer friend was here you've been different. You looked forward to his visit as if he'd been your lover!"

"How dare you!" she screamed. "How dare you say that!"

Her hand flashed out and caught him a stinging blow on the cheek.

"You little vixen!" He caught her violently by the shoulders. "You're driving me to say things I'd no intention of saying!"

"It's better to say what's on your mind than let it rankle!" she panted. "I'm tired of all the insinuations I've had to put up with since I've been here. Piers was never my lover and you know it! I admire him because I admire any man who stands on his own feet and makes something of himself. I'm proud to have worked with him and –"

"And you'd have liked to go on working with him if it hadn't been for the baby, wouldn't you?" he demanded hoarsely. "What a pity your accident didn't happen a little earlier, then you'd have been free to dance in his damn ballet!"

The colour drained from Lucie's face leaving it pinched and ugly. "You can't mean such a horrible thing, Julian. You don't know what you're saying."

Slowly, like an old man, Julian sat down and buried his head in his hands. "I'm sorry, Lucie. Forgive me."

"It isn't a matter of forgiveness, Julian. It goes much deeper than that. Do you really believe I had an accident on purpose – that I wanted to lose the baby so I could go back to the ballet?"

For a long while there was silence. "I don't know what to believe, Lucie," he said at last. "I only wish I did."

There was no reply, and when he raised his head he was alone in the room.

After Julian's accusation Lucie turned instinctively to Ann. Opening the front door of Mayfields some twenty minutes later Ann was taken aback to find her there, so distraught and breathless that she immediately helped her in.

"Good heavens, Lucie, what's the matter?"

"I – I –"

"No, don't talk now, you look all in. Come and sit down and get your breath back."

She propelled Lucie into the lounge and waited until the girl was seated in an armchair with a brandy and soda in her hand before she spoke again.

"Now then, what's happened?"

"I've had a terrible quarrel with Julian."

"Oh, you'll soon patch that up," Ann answered more laconically than she felt. "Francis and I rowed awfully the first year we were married. Drink your brandy and you'll feel better."

With a shaking hand Lucie did as she was told.

"Care to tell me about it?" Ann prompted.

"I'd rather think things out alone, first. I'm sorry – that sounds horribly rude, but –"

"Not at all. I know what you mean. Why not stay the night?"

"Could I?" Lucie asked eagerly. "If only I don't have to see Julian until I've had a chance to think."

"Then it's settled. We've a nice little spare room that's never been slept in and you can be our first guest."

"Oh, Ann, I don't know what I'd do without you."

"Fiddlesticks!" Ann said brusquely. "Don't cry any more, or you'll have me weeping too. Run along and get into bed. It won't do you any harm to have an early night."

"What will Francis say when he knows I'm here?"

"I'll tell him it's something to do with his mother and he'll shut up like a clam! Now run along upstairs and I'll bring your supper up on a tray."

Although determined not to see Julian until she had decided what to do, Lucie hoped against hope that he would come to Mayfields. But Friday night passed, and Saturday and Sunday, with nothing except a phone call to Ann to find out if she was there.

"Didn't he ask to speak to me?"

"No, my dear, but I wouldn't worry about it. Julian can be damned obstinate when he's roused. I don't know the reason you quarrelled, but it must have been serious for you to run away, and he's probably waiting for you to go back first before he makes any move."

Lucie's mouth set. "He can wait."

But although she was sure she was doing the right thing, the weekend would have been unendurable had it not been for Ann's determined cheerfulness and the children's innocent high spirits. It was only after dinner on Sunday evening when Francis had gone to Combe House as usual and the hands of the clock veered past eight, that Lucie knew Julian had returned to

London without getting in touch with her. She needed no prompting then to tell Ann what had happened.

"Francis has said some pretty mean things to me," Ann said, when the cold little voice had stopped, "but he's never gone as far as that. I wouldn't have believed it of Julian. I'm not making excuses for him Lucie, but I don't think he thought that one up on his own. It was a diabolical thing to say, but that's what you're up against – the diabolical influence behind him. I warned you from the start."

"But what could I have done? I tried to make Julian see the way things were going, but he wouldn't."

"And so long as you stay at Combe House he never will."

"Staying at Combe House doesn't enter into it any longer. It's a question of whether I remain with him at all."

"I see. I didn't realise you'd got as far as that. Does Julian know?"

"He must do, unless he thinks I can forget what he said. When I remember how much I wanted the baby, how I looked forward to it during those awful long months –" She broke off, fumbling for a handkerchief, and Ann turned away.

"Perhaps if Julian had been able to see you with Amanda more often, he wouldn't have listened to his mother in the first place."

"I can't believe that even *she* would go to such lengths to part us."

Ann's expression was grim. "She'd stop at nothing to get her sons back."

Neither of them spoke and the silence of the room was broken only by the fat ticking of the grandfather clock. Then Ann bent and switched on the electric fire.

"We may as well be warm even if we're miserable," she said ironically. "You know, Lucie, I was like you when I got married – perhaps a little less soft, but fundamentally just as believing. I had such high hopes of our marriage – Francis was going to do so much and go so far. I thought he'd end up in the Cabinet at least!" She laughed bitterly. "He was going to stand for Parliament, you know, and we were to live in London. Only his mother was afraid that if he left home she wouldn't be able to see him, and persuaded him to look after the estate instead."

"I never knew that." Lucie was surprised. "How awful for

you! You'd think if she really loved her sons she'd want them to be successful."

"Only as long as their success doesn't take them away from her."

"But she knows Julian will eventually go abroad."

"Yes, my dear, but if he has no wife she can go with him. That's why she put an end to Francis's ambitions, only he committed the cardinal sin of getting married to a wife who refused to be ousted. Looking at my husband now, you wouldn't think he was once an intelligent, responsible human being, but he was while he was away from his mother. She seems to paralyse him, as if he's afraid she won't approve of the next breath he draws."

"If you feel like that, why don't you do something?"

"Don't you think I've tried everything I can think of?"

"Perhaps if you left him it might bring him to his senses."

"If I did he'd sink into a morass of self-pity, and she'd make sure he never came after me. Anyway, there are the children. If it hadn't been for them I'd have gone ages ago. I don't love Francis any more, Lucie, but my love didn't die quickly. It was a slow, painful process, and by the time I'd woken up to the fact that it was dead, the children were beginning to grow up."

"Couldn't you take them away with you?"

"I haven't found it in my heart to part them from their father. They adore him. He's wonderful with them, just like an overgrown child himself."

"I don't think I could sacrifice everything for the sake of my children," Lucie said slowly. "I wouldn't have the strength of mind. If only Julian and I had been together all the time I'm sure everything would have been all right!"

Ann stubbed out her cigarette. "Why don't you just go? Surely he couldn't refuse if you insisted?"

"He doesn't think I'm capable of looking after Amanda and I've no intention of leaving her at Combe House with Nurse Richards. As it is, they guard her like a prisoner. Can you imagine how it would be if I only saw her at weekends! No, my only hope is to take Amanda with me. Perhaps that'll bring Julian to his senses."

"Wouldn't that be a little too drastic?"

"I haven't any choice. As long as we stay at Combe House

I'm a shadow behind his mother in his mother's home. Why, he doesn't even treat me as his wife! I'm a child to him, a plaything, and as long as I stay there I'll never be anything else. My only hope is to get out!"

"I wish I had your courage, Lucie," Ann said quietly. "Simon and I are in love with each other."

Lucie stared. "I never guessed – I thought you didn't like him. You've always been so rude, so –"

"Because I was afraid of giving myself away. But walking back to Mayfields after I left you the other day I met him and we – we just fell into each other's arms. I didn't realise till then that he loved me and I'd been tormenting myself – and him – for over a year."

"Oh, Ann dear!"

Ann's eyes shone. "I don't mind. Loving Simon and knowing he loves me has made me happier than I've ever been in my life."

"What are you going to do?"

"What can I do? Conscience won't let me take the twins away from Francis, and I love them too much to leave them behind. Oh, Lucie, I don't know what to do!" She brushed a hand across her eyes and Lucie put her arms around her, unable to offer any solution or advice.

The following morning Lucie went in to breakfast to find Francis still at the table. Usually he was out before she came down, and he regarded her with a half-embarrassed grin.

"Feeling better, old girl?"

"Yes, thank you." She seated herself as Ann came in with a dish of sizzling bacon which she planked down in front of her husband. Francis helped himself liberally and for a few moments there was silence.

"Got a busy morning ahead, so I have to stoke up," he said conversationally as he swallowed his last mouthful. "Incidentally, Ann, I won't be in to lunch."

"Having it with Mother as usual?"

"Yes. Her car's out of order, and I've promised to drive her into Teincombe to do her shopping."

"Since when have you been a part-time chauffeur as well as a –"

"Now, now, don't start nagging in front of Lucie, old girl – you'll set a bad example." Quite unruffled, he drained his cup, and with a cheery good-bye strode out of the room.

Ann stirred her coffee viciously. "Sometimes I think I'll go mad!"

For the first time since her arrival at Mayfields Lucie smiled. "If it wasn't so tragic it'd be funny."

A slow grin spread over Ann's features and she relaxed. "If only we could laugh at the things that annoy us, how much happier we'd be!"

Lucie did not return to Combe House until she was certain her mother-in-law had left for Teincombe, and Ann walked with her as far as the end of the drive.

"Shall I come in and give you a hand? If you want to catch the three-twenty you've got an awful lot to do."

"It's sweet of you to offer, Ann, but I'm not going to implicate you in this. Whatever else Mrs. Summerford says, don't give her a chance to accuse you of helping to break up my marriage."

"I don't give a damn what she says, but perhaps you're right." Impulsively Ann hugged her. "Good-bye, my dear, and good luck. I hope this does the trick for you."

Lucie's mouth was trembling as she walked up the drive and into the house. It had been easy to tell Ann that she was going to leave Combe House with Amanda, but not so easy now that the actual time had come. What would Julian think when he discovered she had gone? Would her action drive them further apart or would it make him realise all she meant to him? Time alone would tell. She had made her decision and there was no going back.

She reached her room without being seen and locked her door before she started to pack. At the end of fifteen minutes she straightened her back with a sigh. Now for Amanda!

A flush rose into Nurse Richards' sallow cheeks when Lucie told her she wanted to take the baby out. But although the thin lips straightened mutinously, the woman said nothing and went down into the garden to fetch her charge.

As soon as she was alone in the nursery Lucie collected as many of Amanda's clothes as she could, running into her own room with them and dumping them in a case. She was able to do this twice before she heard the nurse coming up the stairs, and was standing composedly by the nursery door as she came into view.

"I'll be back for Amanda in about ten minutes."

"Very good, madam."

Lucie went into her room to dial for a taxi, and had struggled down with her cases by the time it drew up at the door.

"I want to catch the three-twenty to London," she said breathlessly. "Do you think we can make it?"

"Oi'll do my best," the driver grinned, "but b'aint no good hurrying too quick round they'm bends. Don't 'ee worry, though, Oi'll get ee thar in toime."

Swiftly she ran upstairs to fetch Amanda, refusing Nurse Richards' offer to carry her down. It would certainly not do for the woman to see all the cases, and by the time she discovered Amanda's clothes were missing they would both be on the Lodon train.

True to his word the taxi-driver deposited her at the station just as the train steamed in, and within minutes she and Amanda were sitting in a carriage with their luggage safely in the guard's van. But it was not until they began to move out of Shalford that she settled back in her corner and breathed a sigh of relief.

She had wired her arrival to Mrs. Cromarty, the landlady with whom she had boarded before her marriage, and knew that however full the house there would always be room for her and Amanda. The baby lay peacefully sucking her thumb, and for a few minutes Lucie hugged her to her breast. For the first time Amanda was dependent on her!

Looking down at the rosy face she was overcome by the enormity of her action. She was banking everything on the hope that Julian would come after her, and refused to contemplate what would happen if he didn't. It was too late now for regrets, the step she had taken was an irrevocable one and there was no turning back.

The street lamps were shedding ghost-blue pools of light when Lucie arrived in Bayswater, so tired and dishevelled that Mrs. Cromarty immediately pillowed her on her ample bosom.

"There now, dearie, what a lovely surprise to see you! And the baby as well? Why, she's the spitting image o' you!"

Amanda promptly began to cry and Lucie sank on a chair in the dark, brown hall.

"She hasn't had her six o'clock feed yet. I forgot to bring her bottle."

"Never mind, ducks, come into the kitchen and I'll see what I can find."

Taking the child in her arms, Mrs. Cromarty led the way down a flight of stairs into the large, cheerful kitchen. "Now sit down and keep an eye on her while I run upstairs. I've still got some of my Carol's baby's things in the attic and I wouldn't be surprised if there's a bottle among 'em."

By this time Amanda was yelling lustily, and looking down into the scarlet face Lucie wished that she could give vent to her feelings in the same way. But by eight o'clock the baby was peacefully asleep in a large drawer lined with blankets and the two women settled down to a cup of tea.

Mrs. Cromarty stirred vigorously. "I think we'll put her in my room for tonight, dearie – I've got to be up early anyway, and you look all in."

At this final display of consideration Lucie emulated her daughter and burst into tears.

"There, there," the landlady soothed. "Don't take on so. Tell old Cromarty what's up."

Lucie wiped her eyes. "I'm sorry to make such a fool of myself, but just being here is so wonderful. This is the first time I've ever had Amanda on my own, and I don't know what I'd have done without you."

"Well, I've brought up five, so it comes natural. You can leave 'er to me until you've made other arrangements. Will you be going out to work again, dearie?"

"I don't think so."

"In that case I can show you 'ow to look after 'er yourself. Sorry I jumped to the wrong conclusion, but seeing you 'ere like this I thought you'd left your old man."

"I have, but I'm hoping he'll come after me." How lame it sounded, put like that!

Mrs. Cromarty sniffed. "Most of us 'opes that, but it don't often 'appen. No good talking about it, you'll know soon enough. I've got your old room ready for you and you can go up when you're ready. You know the way. Come down for a bit to eat when you've 'ad a wash – no good sitting up there brooding."

Lucie settled down with Mrs. Cromarty as if she had never been away. In spite of the smell of cabbage in the passages and the pokiness of her dark little bedroom, this was more her home than the luxurious impersonality of Combe House. And how wonderful was Ma's red, perspiring face from the calm, expressionless rectitude of her mother-in-law!

She spent the whole of the following day by the telephone, but the hours went by and Julian did not ring. It was not until the evening that she began to wonder whether Mrs. Summerford had told Julian she had run away. Perhaps her mother-in-law wanted her to think that Julian did not intend to get in touch with her? Yet to telephone him herself would seem like an admission of defeat – almost as if she regretted running away – and the only thing she could do was to wait for him to make some move towards her.

Three days passed; the longest three days of her life. Days fraught with indecision when the telephone drew her like a magnet and the longing to confide in someone was unbearable. By Saturday she could contain herself no longer, and telephoned the theatre to speak to Piers.

On her return to Combe House Mrs. Summerford was met by an agitated Nurse.

"Amanda's gone!" the woman cried hysterically.

"Gone?" Mrs. Summerford drew off her gloves. "Gone where?"

"With Mrs. Julian. She's run away with her, that's what she's done! She's a wicked young woman – wicked and sly!"

"That's enough, Nurse! Calm yourself and tell me exactly what happened."

With an effort Nurse Richards did as she was told. When she had finished speaking Mrs. Summerford threw down her gloves angrily.

"Do you mean you let her take the baby's clothes under your very nose?"

"She must have taken them when I went to fetch Amanda from her pram. Oh, madam, I wouldn't have had this happen for the world! But I thought she was just taking her to Mayfields, like she did before."

"What time does the London train go?"

"Three-twenty. I've already phoned the station and they said a fair lady and a baby were on it."

"I see. Then there's nothing we can do. You can go now, Nurse. I'll speak to you later."

Crestfallen, Nurse Richards moved away, but half-way up the stairs she turned. "Shall I leave, Mrs. Summerford, or will Amanda be coming back?"

"You can rest assured the baby will be back."

For the next hour Mrs. Summerford sat calmly in the drawing-room and considered the best line of action. Eventually she decided not to get in touch with Julian. If Lucie had run away in the hope of frightening him into letting her live in London she would obviously wait for him to get in touch with her, and it would serve her right to have to cool her heels for a few days. If on the other hand her daughter-in-law had gone direct to Julian there was nothing she could do about it, and Julian himself would telephone her as soon as he had seen Lucie.

But there was no word from him that evening or for the rest of the week and Mrs. Summerford calmly carried out her resolve not to inform him of what had happened until Lucie had suffered for her action.

Julian meanwhile was beginning to be ashamed of the things he had said to Lucie. He had purposely left her alone at Mayfields, afraid that seeing her again would result in another quarrel. But a week in London had cooled his anger and he longed to take her in his arms and by their very physical nearness obliterate everything that had happened. It was easy to misinterpret motives and reactions when one was in love, and he determined that during the coming weekend he would make an honest effort to see her point of view, to find out how she felt and what was going on in her mind – above all, to try and heal the breach that had opened between them.

As soon as he arrived home the following Friday he hurried upstairs to the bedroom, too eager to find Lucie to remember that he had not seen his mother first. The room was empty and he tapped on the bathroom door – perhaps she was changing for dinner – but there was no answer and he looked around him, puzzled at the quiet and bareness. On an impulse he opened the wardrobe and saw the coat-hangers swinging on the rail. The dressing-table was denuded of her things and the photographs they had taken on their honeymoon had disappeared from the chest of drawers, leaving a blank space that filled him with apprehension.

With a muttered exclamation he ran down to the drawing-room. His mother was sitting knitting.

"Why, Julian, I didn't know you'd arrived." She held up her face for his kiss.

"Mother, where's Lucie?"

"Sit down, darling, and I'll tell you."

"What is it? For heaven's sake don't humour me! Just tell me where Lucie is."

"She's gone, dear. She went to London with the baby last Monday afternoon."

"Good God!" He stared at her incredulously. "Why didn't you get in touch with me? You'd no right not to let me know."

He stood up as if he were going to leave that very moment and Mrs. Summerford put her hand on his arm.

"Listen to me first, Julian. If Lucie's gone to London, as we know she has, she's perfectly all right. All her friends are there, and although she may be uncontrolled and hysterical I'm sure she'll see that Amanda's looked after."

"That's beside the point. You should have telephoned me immediately. Really, Mother, I don't know why you took the matter into your hands!"

"Because I wanted you to be perfectly sure you knew what you were doing before you went after her. I put your happiness above everything, Julian – even my own – and I want you to think carefully before you do anything. Lucie's obviously gone to London in the hope of forcing you to let her and Amanda live with you there. That's a form of blackmail unworthy of a decent wife and if you'd run to heel as soon as you had heard she'd gone, you would never be master in your own home again. I don't think it'll do her any harm to realise you can't be brow-beaten into giving in to her."

Julian stood up again and paced the room. "I know you've done everything for the best, Mother, but you've gone a bit too far this time. Lucie's my wife and I must make my own decisions about her."

"Being forced to do things is hardly making your own decisions."

"The position between us is too strained for me to stand on my dignity. If I do I'll find my marriage in ruins." He lit a cigarette. "I've got a pretty good idea where she is. She's probably gone back to the boarding-house where she lived before we were married."

"Or to Mr. Bellamy?"

"Mother!"

"I'm sorry to hurt you, darling, but it's better to face facts before it's too late. Heaven knows I don't want it to be true, but I feel it my duty to warn you that she may have run away because she wants to be with that dancer."

"I see," he said quietly. "Then the only way to prove you're wrong is to go to London and find out. I shall drive up first thing in the morning."

They spoke little that evening and for the first time Julian could remember the atmosphere between him and his mother was constrained. But when he went down at seven o'clock the following morning it was to find her already dressed and having breakfast.

She smiled at his expression of surprise. "I'm coming with you, Julian. I won't let you go to London on your own."

"There's really no need."

"But I want to come. I feel Lucie may be blaming me, and if you're going to start your marriage again we must all be open with our grievances. It's no good building a relationship on misunderstandings."

He was deeply touched. "Thank you, Mother! I'm sorry I was so rude last night."

"That's all right, darling, it was my fault. I just want whatever's best for you, and if you still feel your happiness lies with Lucie. . . ."

They arrived at Paddington early in the afternoon and immediately took a taxi to Bayswater, drawing up outside the greystone house where he had called for Lucie so many times in the past.

He knocked loudly on the shiny brass knocker and the door

was opened by a thin little girl in a navy school tunic.

"Can I see Mrs. Summerford?" he asked. The name obviously meant nothing and he tried again. "Are you the landlady's daughter?"

"No, she's my grandma."

"Who's at the door, Carol?" Mrs. Cromarty waddled into view. "Why, it's Lucie's husband, ain't it? How are you?"

"Quite well, thank you. I've come to see my wife. Is she here?"

"Not right now, but you come in and wait."

She held the door wide and Mrs. Summerford and Julian followed her down the hall into the parlour, perching themselves uncomfortably on the hard edge of a shiny sofa.

"Lucie *is* staying with you, then?" Julian asked pointedly.

"She is. Would you be wanting to patch it up?"

"That hardly concerns you," Mrs. Summerford put in.

Julian laid a hand on her arm. "Let me talk, Mother. I've come to take my wife home – where she belongs."

"Well, you'll have to wait a bit. You only missed her by a few minutes."

"Is she out with the baby?"

"No, the little girl's 'ere. Ever such a sweet thing she is too, just like Lucie. And so good, you wouldn't know she was in the 'ouse. You've got a kid to be proud of, sir."

"Thank you. Do you know what time my wife will be back?"

"Can't say for sure. I told her I'd feed the baby if Piers wanted 'er to stay on."

"Piers?" Julian's voice was sharp.

"Yes – the dancer fellow. She's gone to his matinée this afternoon, so I thought as 'ow she might stay on and 'ave a bite to eat with him after the show."

For a moment Julian was at a loss, and Mrs. Summerford leaned forward quickly. "Is this the first time my daughter-in-law has seen Mr. Bellamy, Mrs. Cromarty?"

"Oh, no. He was 'ere the other night to cheer 'er up. Ever so depressed she was. But it's the first time she's been round to the theatre."

"Ah." There was a wealth of meaning in his mother's voice and Julian flinched.

"I wish to take Amanda home," he said to the landlady.

"Please get her ready."

Mrs. Cromarty was taken aback. "Lucie put 'er in my care, sir, and I don't know whether –"

"It will be quite all right," Mrs. Summerford put in, "we'll pick Lucie up at the theatre."

"Well, in that case I suppose it's all right," Mrs. Cromarty smiled. "If you'll just wait a minute I'll get the baby ready. She's 'aving 'er afternoon nap, but it won't take me long."

She went away and mother and son sat together in silence until she returned with a white woolly bundle, which she placed unceremoniously in Julian's arms. " 'Ere she is. Sweet, ain't she?"

It was the first time Julian had ever held his daughter. At birth she had been too frail to be handled and as soon as Nurse Richards had taken charge she had made him feel incapable of holding the child at all. Now, looking down into the small, rosy face and listening to the quick, shallow breathing, he was filled with a passionate indignation that Lucie should have subjected this defenceless little creature to risks and insecurity.

"Come along, Julian, we mustn't waste time," his mother said briskly.

They bade the genial landlady good-bye and within a few minutes were in a taxi on their way back to Paddington. They were nearing the station before Julian broke the silence.

"I owe you an apology, Mother. It's perfectly obvious now that everything you've said about Lucie is true."

As if she realized this was not the time for words, Mrs. Summerford looked down at the sleeping baby and said nothing.

When Lucie returned to the boarding-house late that afternoon Mrs. Cromarty regarded her as if she were a ghost.

"Lord, duckie! Have you missed 'em?"

"Missed whom?"

"Your 'usband and 'is mother. They came 'ere this afternoon and when they 'eard you was out they asked to take the baby and said they'd pick you up at the theatre."

"You didn't give her to them, did you? You didn't let them take her away?" Mrs. Cromarty nodded and the colour drained from Lucie's face. "Why didn't you ring me at the theatre? Oh, Ma, you shouldn't have believed them!"

"But it was what you've been waiting for, wasn't it? When the old girl said they'd call for you I thought it was sure to be all right. Oh, Lucie ducks, what've I done?"

She tried to pull the girl towards her, but Lucie wrenched herself free. "What a fool I was to go out! I should have known they'd do something like this. Why didn't I stay with Amanda? Why did I have to go to the theatre the very afternoon they came? Oh, Ma, they've taken my baby!" She began to cry uncontrollably. "They don't know what they've done to me, Ma! How could they be so cruel? Amanda's mine, she's mine – I nearly died for her! Oh, what shall I do, what shall I do?"

She collapsed against the stairs, sobbing as if her heart would break, and Mrs. Cromarty stood by helplessly, the tears pouring down her cheeks and smearing the orange powder on her raddled face.

Suddenly Lucie straightened up. "I must go to Piers!" she said wildly. "He'll know what to do, he'll help me."

"Let me make you a cup of tea first, dearie. It'll make you feel better. I'll put the kettle on and it'll be ready in a jiffy."

"No, Ma, I couldn't drink anything. I must see Piers right away. He'll tell me how to get Amanda back. He'll help me."

Piers was resting in his dressing-room before the evening performance when Lucie burst in. "They've taken Amanda!" she cried. "They called at Ma Cromarty's while I was here and took her away! Oh, Piers, you've got to help me! Tell me how to get her back – I've no one else to turn to."

She seemed on the verge of collapse, her pale face flushed and damp, her eyes wild. He caught her against him and rocked her backwards and forwards as if she herself was a baby.

"Hush, Lucie, don't cry. It won't do you any good and it won't bring Amanda back . . . Lucie, my dear, take a hold of yourself, you'll make yourself ill." He drew her to the couch in the corner and waited until her sobs had ceased. "There, that's better. Now wipe your eyes and stop looking so miserable."

She gave him a watery smile. "I'm sorry to be such a nuisance, Piers, but it was such a shock I didn't know what to do."

"I don't think there's much you *can* do."

"But Amanda's mine!"

"Not in the eyes of the law. I'm not absolutely sure of my

facts, but I've an idea that when you ran away from Julian you put yourself in the wrong."

"But I didn't run away from *him*," she cried. "I only ran away from Combe House because I thought he'd follow me."

Piers still looked unconvinced. "The best thing is to go and see a lawyer on Monday. He'll be able to advise you much better than I can."

"Monday! But I want to know right away! They've taken my baby away from me, Piers, don't you understand?"

"It's your husband's baby too," he reminded her gently.

"Julian's hardly noticed her up to now. It's his mother who's behind this. She made him do it, so she'll have charge of Amanda – she and that hateful nurse!" She began to cry again and Piers gently stroked her hair.

"Crying won't get you anywhere, darling. I tell you what – we'll drop in and see Charles Blackmer on our way home. He's Dennison's lawyer, so he's used to being woken up at all hours by the old man. If you like I'll give him a ring and tell him to expect us – he won't mind seeing us after the show."

"Oh, Piers, will you?"

"Of course. Now come along downstairs and have a cup of coffee before the curtain goes up. Watch from the wings tonight, Lucie, it'll take your mind off things. Time enough to worry when we hear what Blackmer has to say."

Lucie wiped her eyes. "I don't know what I'd have done if it hadn't been for you."

"Nonsense. If you can't turn to me when you need someone, what's a friend for? Now buck up, darling. Things are never as bad as they seem."

But Lucie felt anything but cheerful as, later that evening, she followed Piers into the book-lined study of Charles Blackmer's flat off the Strand, and a small, plump man rose to greet them.

"Hullo, Piers, what can I do for you? Having trouble with Dennison?"

"Not this time," the dancer grinned. "It's Lucie Marlow – pardon me – Lucie Summerford. She's in a spot of matrimonial trouble and I thought you'd be able to help her."

"Of course. What's it all about?" He sat down, his small, tubby body relaxed in a large wing-back chair, his hands crossed over his stomach and his feet barely touching the floor.

Briefly and as unemotionally as she could, Lucie told him of the events that had led up to her leaving Combe House, and the little man leaned back and put his finger-tips together.

"An unfortunate story, but not an unusual one. If I had as many pounds as the number of marriages that have gone on the rocks through mothers-in-law I'd be a rich man. I take it you want to know whether you can get your child back?"

"Yes." Lucie leaned forward in her chair.

"Well, I'm afraid it isn't going to be easy." He stood up and poured himself a drink from a carafe of water. "In an English marriage the husband has equal claim to any offspring unless he happens to be the guilty party, which is not the case here. As far as I can make out your marriage was incompatible for divers reasons, and I think you should face the fact that you've forfeited any right to your child by running away. I'm sorry to put it so bluntly, but it's as well if you know where you stand."

"You mean I won't ever be able to have Amanda again?"

"I wouldn't say that, but I doubt if any court would give you full custody."

"But I'm her mother . . ."

"The law doesn't deal with emotional issues, my dear, only with cold facts. And whatever way you look at it your husband has more advantages to offer the child than you. You aren't even in a position to look after her adequately – if you were, it might be worth trying to get custody for part of each year."

"What would happen if Lucie got a divorce?" Piers asked suddenly.

Lucie looked round quickly. "Oh, Piers, I hadn't even thought about that!"

"I'm only asking as a point of interest," he said gently. He looked at the lawyer. "Would it make any difference if she were legally separated from her husband?"

"Only if she were in a better financial position. At the moment she can't support herself, let alone a child!"

There was quiet in the room, the hum of distant traffic muted and soft through the thick plush curtains. Lucie was the first to speak.

"It seems that money can buy all things, even your own child. What can I do? I'm not trained for anything except dancing, and I haven't even done that for over a year."

"I'm sure Dennison will take you back again," Piers said quietly.

Lucie did not reply but stood up and held out her hand. "Thank you for seeing me, Mr. Blackmer."

Blackmer shook his head. "I'm sorry my advice wasn't more palatable. Don't hesitate to call on me again if there's anything else you want to know." He escorted them to the door. "By the way, Piers, ask Jack Dennison to pop in and have a word with me some time this week, will you? There's a clause in the American contract I don't like very much. Incidentally, when are you going?"

"In a couple of months. One of his friends in Florida has invited the company to stay with him and do our final rehearsals there."

"Dennison must be delighted," Blackmer grinned, "it'll save him such a lot of expense!"

In the ensuing days Lucie clung to the hope that Julian might get in touch with her, but the weekend came round again and her only message from him was a communication from his solicitors asking her to call and see them.

Unlike Mr. Blackmer, Julian's solicitor was terse to the point of rudeness.

"You realise, Mrs. Summerford, that my client cannot take steps to divorce you until you've been married three years."

Until then Lucie had not grasped the full implication of her position. Now, hearing this austere man talk so glibly about divorce she realised how completely Julian had misinterpreted her running away, how easily he had jumped to the wrong conclusion. Pride forbade her making an excuse. By his very willingness to believe the worst of her, Julian had clearly shown his attitude.

"What about my baby?" she managed to ask.

"Mr. Summerford is willing for you to see her whenever you wish."

"But I want her with me!"

"I'm afraid there's no possibility of that. As these cases go, your husband is being generous in allowing you access to her at all."

"But he knows very well I can't afford to keep going down to Devon!"

"My client is willing to give you an allowance until such time as he can petition for a divorce. Of course, you are not entitled to this, but – ahem – Mr. Summerford is prepared in the –"

"Julian can keep his money – I don't want it! I only want to know how long he intends to keep Amanda in Devon?"

"I understand the child will remain there until such time as Mr. Summerford has a home of his own."

"A home of his own!" she said bitterly. "If my husband had had a home of his own our marriage would never have come to this."

The lawyer looked faintly affronted at her outburst and Lucie got to her feet.

"Thank my husband for his generosity in allowing me to see my child, but I want more than a monthly or weekly visit. If he won't let me have her I must wait until I'm in a position to fight for her."

"You're setting yourself a difficult task," the solicitor said drily, "but as a mother I don't suppose you can see that."

"I've seen what the power of a mother can do," Lucie replied. "Now it's my turn to use it. Good morning."

CHAPTER VI

JULIAN was shattered by the discovery that Lucie had gone to Piers and Mrs. Summerford took the reins quietly into her own hands. Nurse Richards received her charge with infinite satisfaction, and obeyed her employer's orders to keep Amanda out of the way. A discreet talk with Lady Ranken obtained a few days' leave of absence for Julian and Mrs. Summerford saw to it that he was kept occupied on the estate.

"You may as well see everything's going as well as possible here, darling, in case you decide to ask Sir John to send you abroad."

"I can't very well do that, Mother, I've already been assigned to the Swedish Legation in London."

"Perhaps Sir John might change his mind. It'll be awkward for you to stay in London with Lucie there."

"Not at all," he retorted irritably. "I was in London for years before I met Lucie and there's no reason why I should meet her now."

"You needn't lose your temper, Julian."

"I'm sorry," he apologised, "I – I'll get over it soon."

"I'm sure you will, darling. As long as you want to."

"As long as you want to." But did he want to? He had told his mother that Lucie no longer meant anything to him, yet he had not been speaking the truth. You could not turn love on and off like a tap – indeed his own emotion was more like a geyser, gushing forth anger and jealousy and love in one continuous stream. Such emotion could not be suppressed no matter how hard he tried; it must dry up of its own accord.

His mother was so sure she was right in condemning Lucie that he was carried along on the strength of her conviction. It was only later, days later, that he wondered whether he had been right in taking the baby without waiting to hear what Lucie had to say. By then it was too late. His solicitor informed him that Lucie had refused his offer of maintenance – an offer he had made principally to avoid his wife being dependent on another man – and read into her refusal a desire to sever the last link between them.

At the end of a fortnight he returned to London to take up his new appointment. Many times during the next few months he was tempted to get in touch with Lucie, and hoped against hope that if she went down to see Amanda he would be home when she did so. It was terrible to be so near yet not see her, terrible to long for her in spite of his disgust at what she had done. But summer gave way to autumn and she still did not visit Combe House.

In London meanwhile Lucie worked so feverishly that even Piers remonstrated.

"You can't force your strength back too quickly, Lucie, it's a gradual process."

"But Jack won't take me on the tour if I'm not ready, and I can't stay behind."

"Don't worry about that. You'll go with us all right."

She turned away from the barre. "You're very good to me, Piers. Why are you taking so much trouble?"

"Two reasons," he smiled. "One, because I think you have it in you to be a very good dancer, and the other . . ."

"The other?"

"Because I'm fond of you."

Her face softened. "I'm fond of you too, Piers. You've been a wonderful friend."

"What a rewarding thing to hear! D'you know, it's the first time I've liked a woman calling me her friend? Now come on, up on your points." Their rehearsal continued.

Although Lucie longed to see Amanda she knew it would be folly to go down to Devon in her present state of mind. To see her mother-in-law now would destroy the hard-won self-control which was so necessary to her work. Better to wait until the possibility of having Amanda back was not so entirely out of reach. To make money she must work, to work she must be able to concentrate, and it was ironical that her very love for Amanda might be an obstacle to her career – a career she had taken up again almost entirely for the child's sake.

As soon as she had settled down, Lucie wrote and told Ann everything that had happened, and by return of post received a long letter agreeing with her reason for not going down to Combe House.

"I see Mandy in Shalford now and then with that awful Nurse and she's so lovely that I feel you're wise not to upset yourself by seeing her. The position between Francis and myself is still unchanged, but I'm getting more and more restless. Perhaps it's because you had the courage to get out and I haven't. If only Robert and Richard weren't so dependent on me! God knows it must be hard enough to leave a child Amanda's age, but the boys bring all their troubles to me, and it's more than I can do to leave them. Simon is wonderful. He knows I'm desperately unhappy but never tries to force me into a decision, although I don't think we can go on like this much longer. Still, I don't want to worry you with my troubles – I'm sure you have enough of your own, and I can't tell you how sorry I am that things have turned out the way they have."

Gradually the month drew to a close, and Lucie's muscles became more pliant and supple. Early every morning she practised with Piers before going to the classroom for the daily work-over with the rest of the company.

Lucie had expected her year's absence to set her back, and hoped that hard work would hasten her recovery. But she was to learn that the body could not be hurried, as Piers had warned her, and aching limbs and bulging thighs were the only outcome of too much practice in too short a time. Her hope that she might soon reach the stage of development at which she had left was soon dashed, for Dennison told her bluntly that it would be a long time before she was fit to tackle the solos she had been doing before she had left the company. She knew he was difficult to please, but hoped his severity was the outcome of his annoyance at her desertion rather than her own ineptitude, and realized that only by dogged determination could she convince him of the sincerity of her desire to make amends.

As the date of their departure drew near Lucie knew she could not leave England without seeing Amanda. There was no girl-friend with whom she could discuss her problems for her year's absence had set her a little apart from the rest of the corps de ballet; Piers was the only one she could turn to, and when she told him she was going to see Amanda he regarded her questioningly.

"Why are you telling me? Do you want my opinion or my support?"

"Your honest opinion, Piers. Do you think I should go before we leave for America or should I wait until we come back?"

"Frankly I'd advise you to wait. Seeing Amanda for such a short time won't be any compensation for having to part with her all over again."

"In that case I'll never see her at all!"

"Exactly."

"Piers, how can you be so heartless! Do you expect me to behave as though I'd never had a child?" She moved distractedly round the dressing-room. "I'm not a girl any more. I seem to have become completely maternal since Amanda was born – it even comes between me and dancing. I don't expect you to understand how I feel. It's different for a man and –"

"Men have emotions too," he said sharply. "But if you become obsessed with Amanda you'll never succeed as a dancer, and if you don't succeed you won't be able to fight for her, so it's a vicious circle. You've got to submerge yourself in your work, Lucie. There's no room for anything in your life except dancing."

She laughed mirthlessly. "I thought you once said my dancing was too cold? Surely emotional experience will make me a better artist?"

"Only if you don't let it play havoc with you. You can't go on to a stage and dance out your personal feelings; it won't mean a thing to an audience. Emotional experience can give you greater depth, but you can't use the emotion itself. If you do, your dancing will be merely neurotic."

"I see." She sat down. "You make me sound rather unhealthy."

"On the contrary, you'd be unhealthy if you *didn't* want to see your child. But if you're going to be an artist, you must learn self-control."

"Perhaps I shall become temperamental!"

"Not if you dance with me!" He began to cream off his make-up. "Genuine temperament is an artistic reaction against anything that jars, but the conventional idea of a temperamental ballet dancer is false." He pointed a finger at her. "Don't make the mistake of confusing temper with temperament!"

She smiled at his vehemence. "Then I'd better reserve my tantrums until I'm good enough to get away with them!"

"And I'll reserve the right to put you across my knee!"

"In that case I can see storms ahead." Her smile faded. "All this talk still hasn't solved my problem. Oh, Piers, I don't think I could bear to go to America without seeing Amanda!"

Piers looked at her through the mirror, his expression hidden behind a melting mask of make-up. "As a matter of interest, Lucie – are you going down because you want to see Amanda or because you hope you might see Julian and patch things up?"

She caught her breath. "I knew you were going to ask that. If I had any pride I suppose I'd say yes to the first question and no to the last. But it wouldn't be true, Piers. I suppose I *am* hoping that if Julian and I saw each other again we might try and make a go of things."

"And your dancing – all these months of work? Would you just give it up?"

"I don't honestly know. If Julian and I started again he'd have to love me because I'm me, not in spite of the fact that I'm a dancer. But there's no point in talking about it now – if and when it ever happens will be time enough." She stood up. "What day do we leave?"

"Friday week."

"Then I'd better go to Devon this weekend."

"If you make it Saturday I'll come with you – if you want me to."

"Would you? Would you really?" She ran to his side and caught his arm. "I hate the idea of going alone. If Julian's there it'll be bad enough, but if I have to see my mother-in-law on my own...."

"Don't worry, I'll go with you." He grinned and pushed back his chair. "I hope you appreciate that I'm giving you the one free weekend we've got left? Don't make it too early in the morning – I've been looking forward to a lie-in!"

"Lazy beast, a breath of fresh air will do you good."

He pulled a face. "I hate fresh air!"

During the journey to Shalford Piers' gossip stopped Lucie from thinking, and when the train drew up at Teincombe station it was difficult to believe she had left it four months ago in such a fever of hope and uncertainty.

They stepped into a waiting taxi and rattled along the narrow high street with its deserted, Sundayish air, across the bridge spanning the river, and over to Shalford.

As the cab wound up the hill towards Combe House Lucie's palms grew moist and Piers squeezed her arm.

"It'll soon be over, darling. I'll tell the taxi to wait so we can leave as soon as you're ready. Does Julian know you're coming?"

"I don't know. I don't even know if he'll be there. I wrote to Nurse Richards and told her to have Amanda ready for me – she usually takes her for a walk in the afternoon, so I wanted to make sure she'd be in. Oh, Piers, I wonder if she'll know me?"

"I doubt it, at six months. You'll probably find it difficult to recognise her too. Children change so quickly."

"You know a lot about them?" She was making conversation.

He grinned. "Strange as it may seem, I've a couple of second cousins twice removed – sometimes even ballet dancers are human enough to have relations!"

"You don't have to tell me you're human, Piers."

"Sometimes I wonder."

At that moment the taxi turned out of the lane into the drive and in front of them lay Combe House. How smugly solid it looked, how complacent the smooth lawns and carefully tended beds, the wide windows and long terrace! She had come here as a bride scarcely more than a year ago and now she was returning as an outsider, a mere visitor allowed to enter the sacred portals on sufferance, under the aegis of her mother-in-law's permission. She swallowed and pushed her hair back from her forehead with a trembling hand, but when she stepped out of the taxi she looked calm and determined, her face devoid of any tell-tale emotion.

The tall, narrow door with its beautifully polished knocker was firmly closed, and she rang the bell and heard it echo down the hall before footsteps sounded and Gladys appeared.

Lucie stepped firmly over the threshold. "I believe I'm expected, Gladys. Is Amanda in the nursery?"

"I think so, Mrs. Julian," the maid said uncertainly. "Nurse Richards did say she was letting her stay in for the afternoon."

"Good." Lucie turned to Piers. "We'll go straight up."

Walking down the corridor towards the nursery, Lucie hesitated outside her old bedroom and through the half-open door caught a glimpse of her mother-in-law's hair-brushes lying on the dressing-table. How quickly the house had settled back into its old ways, only Amanda remaining to bear witness to the fact that Julian had ever married and begotten a child! She walked steadily past the room that held so many memories, and with a little rush ran the last few yards and flung open the nursery door.

Amanda was lying on a rug on the floor kicking her legs in the air and gurgling at her own fat, pink toes. For a moment Lucie watched her, then with a little cry she knelt and scooped her up, rocking the small body to and fro as she breathed in the fragrance of talcum powder mingled with the milky odour of babyhood.

Piers cleared his throat discreetly and indicated the balcony outside the nursery windows. "I'll wait out here."

Lucie was scarcely aware of his going and for the next half-hour was completely absorbed in her little girl. Had her eyes always been so grey, the hair so soft and fair as it lay smooth against the beautifully shaped little head? "Mandy, Mandy," she murmured. "My precious Mandy!" Although she realised the baby could not know her, Lucie's heart warmed every time Amanda gave a toothless smile or reached out a chubby hand to pull her hair as she knelt on the carpet, peeping at Amanda through her fingers and making the noises with which every mother amuses her baby. Her shoes slipped off, but she let them lie where they fell, and when the baby reached out for her toes Lucie swept her up in her arms again and hugged her.

The door behind them opened quietly and, suddenly conscious of being watched, Lucie looked up. Julian was standing there and for a moment they stared at each other in silence over the baby's head. His dark suit threw his features into relief, making him seem taller and thinner, and she was reminded of the first time she had met him at Mimi Delfont's party.

She put Amanda down on the rug and scrambled to her feet. "Hullo, Julian, I didn't know you'd be here." She slipped on her shoes, gaining a little confidence from her added height. "I barely recognised Amanda, she's grown so much."

Watching her, Julian wondered if she had always been so slight, always looked so defenceless? Without her shoes she was even smaller than he recollected – such a little thing to hide so much determination and strength of purpose.

"Amanda's made very good progress," he said formally. "Nurse Richards looks after her extremely well."

"Not as well as a mother, but no doubt she's efficient." Lucie's tone was equally formal. She bent and picked the baby up. "Say hullo to Daddy, darling."

Amanda stared at her father and Julian stared back.

"Here, take her."

"No, thanks," he said hastily, "I might drop her or something."

"Of course you won't! Aren't you used to holding her?" He shook his head. "Well, take her now. I've never heard of a father who doesn't like holding his baby."

Before he could move away she placed the child against him and his arms went round the little body involuntarily. Since Lucie had left him he'd scarcely looked at the baby at all. Now, peering into the tiny face, he marvelled that this being was part of him. Strange that his love for Lucie should have created the child he was holding, stranger still that it had not forged a link between them but had become an obstacle in their way, an object of dispute.

"Quite a big girl now, aren't you, Amanda?" he said softly. The baby cooed and smacked his cheek. "Hey, young lady, not so free with your fists!" For answer she smacked him again and his expression was so comical that Lucie laughed and took her away.

"She's learning fast, isn't she? I hope it means she'll be able to look after herself when she grows up." Unwittingly, bitterness crept in.

"Do you think that's such a necessary accomplishment in a woman?" Julian asked quietly.

"I can only speak from experience," she replied. "You have to be able to fight for what you want in this world."

"What *do* you want, Lucie?"

"Why do you ask? I'm not different from any other woman. I want a home and children and a husband who loves me and puts me first."

"And your career?"

"I gave it up willingly to get married because life with the man I loved meant more to me than any success I might have achieved in the ballet."

"But you changed your mind," he countered.

"Do you think so, Julian? Don't you know me better than that?"

"Lucie darling, do you mean –?" He took a step towards her, but as he did so Piers stepped back into the room.

"We'd better go if you want to catch that train, Lucie," he began. Then catching sight of Julian, he stopped. "Good afternoon, Summerford. I hope I'm not intruding."

"Perhaps I should be the one to apologize for intruding?" Julian said icily. "I'd no idea you were out there, Bellamy, or I'd have asked you in to share our happy little domestic scene." He rounded on Lucie. "I didn't expect much of you, but I thought you'd have decency enough to come here alone!"

"Really, Julian, what a boorish thing to say!"

"What do you expect – a speech of welcome?"

Her face flamed. "You might at least be civil instead of behaving like an ill-mannered schoolboy – or is your mother deliberately stopping you from growing up?"

"Kindly leave my mother out of this! You took enough time making up your mind to come and see Amanda, but if you had to bring Bellamy it would have been better if you'd stayed away altogether!"

"Don't talk to Lucie like that!" Piers interrupted angrily.

"I'll talk to my wife as I please – and I'll be pleased if she doesn't come and see Amanda again!"

"You can't stop me coming!" she cried. "You can't stop me, do you hear? If you knew what it's cost me not to come you wouldn't speak to me like this!"

"It's not my fault you haven't been down – I've never stopped you. But perhaps you haven't had time? After all, your life is full of other things now."

"That only shows what little imagination you have! I've wanted to see Amanda more than anything, but –"

"Then you've an odd way of showing your love," he said acidly. "Not content with running away from her, you haven't been near her for months. Is that maternal devotion?"

"I didn't run away from her, you stole her from me!" Lucie's voice rose hysterically and Amanda began to cry. "You stole her from me, you know you did!"

"I'd hardly call it stealing to take my own child home, but then you always did dramatise everything."

"Spoken like a true Summerford – well-bred and cold-blooded to the last!"

"Don't forget Amanda's a Summerford too."

"God help her, so she is! That's one more reason why I'm going to get her away from you."

"You'll find that very difficult, so don't fool yourself into hoping you can." He took a step towards her. "In spite of my being a Summerford, which is something you suddenly seem to despise, I won't prevent you from seeing Amanda entirely, but I've no intention of letting you have her."

"You won't be able to stop me! I've a right to my baby and I'll fight you until I get her back!"

Piers caught her arm. "Don't upset yourself, darling, you'll only suffer for it afterwards."

A spasm of anger passed across Julian's face. "I said I wouldn't stop you seeing Amanda and I meant it. But for decency's sake don't bring your lover next time you come!"

The door closed behind him and Lucie swayed as if she were going to faint. Piers made a move to take her in his arms, but she shook her head and with an obvious effort bent and kissed Amanda, and without a backward glance went out of the room. They walked in silence along the corridor, down the wide sweep of stairs and out to the waiting taxi.

It was not until they were nearly at Paddington that Lucie finally spoke.

"I'm sorry you witnessed such insufferable behaviour, Piers. Your only reward for going with me was to be insulted by my husband."

"It isn't an insult to be thought your lover, Lucie. It was the slur on you that I resented. No one has ever done less to deserve it."

Tears welled into her eyes. "Oh, Piers, I don't know what to say," she began, and looked so tired and distressed that he leant forward and patted her hand.

"Don't worry on my account, you've enough to put up with

already. I was afraid something like this would happen, although even I didn't think Summerford would be quite so – imaginative." She said nothing, and he went on: "I don't like giving advice when it isn't asked, but for your own good I don't think you should see Amanda again until you know you've a chance of getting her back."

Fear animated her face. "Do you think Julian was right when he said I've no hope?"

"I don't know, but Blackmer said you'd stand a better chance if you were in a position to support her."

A tired smile lifted the corners of her mouth. "I don't think any dancer has been fired with ambition for such a good reason as mine. If this doesn't make me a ballerina, nothing will."

CHAPTER VII

It was pouring with rain the day the Dennison Company left England. As Piers took his seat on the plane the place beside him was firmly taken by Adana, the prima ballerina. Only when he realised that he would not have Lucie's company on the long flight did he begin to realise how deep his love for her had gone. Her attitude was so sisterly, so completely devoid of any sexual significance, that he almost despaired of making her conscious of him as a man. Yet he baulked at the idea of rushing her defences, as he had done so often in his life before, and for the first time was willing to wait in the hope that she would eventually turn to him of her own accord.

It was unfortunate that Adana should have suddenly taken a liking to Piers. When he had been merely a dancer he had not interested her, but now that he was gaining a reputation as a choreographer she became acutely conscious of his attractions and set out to make him equally conscious of hers.

Although Piers knew that to ignore her blandishments would make partnering her more difficult than ever, he could not even pretend to like her, for she was arrogant, vain, and bad-tempered. Perhaps if she had been a greater dancer it would have lessened his dislike, but although technically brilliant she was essentially superficial and lacked the ability to convey anything but her own vivid personality to her audience.

It did not take Adana long to discover that Lucie Marlow was the reason for Piers' indifference. If the girl had been beautiful or clever she would not have been so infuriated, but that he should prefer a corps dancer – a small, insignificant creature who had left the company to get married and come back with her tail between her legs – was more than her pride could bear, and she determined to break up their relationship.

Although Lucie had unwittingly made an enemy – and a formidable one at that, she was less unhappy than she had been for some time, for at last she was doing something constructive towards getting Amanda. When she had left Julian the conviction that he still loved her had remained obstinately firm, but his accusation that Piers was her lover had forced upon her how irrevocably they had drifted apart, and she wondered whether she had known the real Julian at all. Her anger gave her a sense of release from him, and where before there had lurked the belief that if she could get Amanda she would get Julian back as well, there was now only a determination to claim her child. Of Julian she had no more hope and, she was tempted to believe, no more love. Her only wish was to make him taste the same bitterness he had forced upon her – above all, to prove to her mother-in-law that she was a person in her own right, ready to fight them with any weapons they chose.

At New York they were met by Dennison's friend and mentor, Simeon Hakenberg, a genial American with a wide-brimmed hat and long cigar, who it was said, had amassed a fortune from the manufacture of sausage skins but had a sincere respect for the arts and in particular the ballet. It was at his home in Florida that the company were to rehearse before their New York debut.

By the time they took off again it was nearly dusk and they had dinner over Washington, eating thick steaks as they looked down at the twinkling lights of the capital. Gradually the hum of conversation subsided and one by one the dancers tilted back their seats and dropped off to sleep, lulled by the steady throb of the engine.

Only Lucie found it hard to settle. Every mile was taking her further away from Amanda and the calm resolution with which she had faced the separation during the sea voyage was suddenly shaken. She would have given anything to be back at Combe House with her baby, anything, as long as they were together.

It was barely six-thirty in the morning when they landed at Miami Airport, but a sultry heat-haze already covered the ground, shimmering the dusty tarmac and accentuating the pearly radiance of the sun. Rubbing the sleep from their eyes, they piled into shooting-brakes and drove through the wide, quiet streets towards Miami Beach – past Lincoln Road with its enormous shops, past the magnificent hotels towering towards the sky – until they drew up at a large white house whose front garden was ablaze with flowers. There was still no sign of the sea and it was only when they trooped into the long hall that they saw it glistening through the glass walls at the far end of the house and realised that the hotels and private residences gave directly on to the beach, hiding it from the eyes of casual visitors and would-be promenaders.

Mr. Hakenberg's home, like Mr. Hakenberg, was large and expansive. The hall led off into a huge lounge, the end wall of which was composed entirely of glass doors thrown open to a wide, mosaic terrace shaded by palm trees overlooking the whitest stretch of sand they had ever seen.

The company settled quickly into a routine. Hakenberg had had long mirrors and a barre set up in the ballroom, the only difference from their London practice-room being that the old piano was replaced by a shiny white grand and through the ever-open french windows they could see the glaring sand and blue sea, lit by brilliant sunshine.

In the afternoons it was too hot to rehearse and the beach in front of the house was strewn with the outstretched bodies of dancers in various stages of nudity. Madame Molina would plod from one group to another anxiously enjoining them to avoid tell-tale sun-tan marks which would show on the stage, but the minute her back was turned off would go the blouses and out would come the sun-tan oil! As soon as the sun went down work was resumed, and it was several hours before the dancers were free to troop wearily upstairs to shower and change for a late dinner before going to bed.

Piers and Lucie were the only exception to this, for they worked together every evening. At first she protested she could practise on her own, but he insisted on helping her, and every night they would rehearse the following day's routine. Piers was already composing a new ballet and used Lucie to help him work out the steps, sometimes adapting them to suit her own personal ability. Gradually her dependence on him increased, and when he berated her for a false step or gesture she felt it was not always Piers the dancer talking but Piers the man – a feeling which grew stronger as the weeks went by.

The first intimation Lucie had of Adana's dislike was when they started rehearsing The Sleeping Beauty and Dennison allowed her to take her old part of the Blue Bird, the only sign of encouragement he had given her since her return. The entire company was assembled in the practice-room when the storm broke.

"I do not think this girl is ready yet!" The ballerina's dark mouth was petulant.

"On the contrary, she is quite ready," Dennison said levelly. "If you remember she danced it two years ago."

"I do not care when she danced it," Adana persisted. "I say she is not good enough."

Dennison's eyes glinted. "My dear Adana, you may be the ballerina of his company, but I am still the ballet-master – you understand?"

"But how can I be a success if I am supported by inferior dancers?"

"It is not only *your* success I am anxious for, but the success of the company as a whole."

Instantly Adana changed her tactics. "But, Jack, *I* have the company's success at heart too – that is why I am so anxious." She turned to Lucie with a charming smile. "I am sure that if you are as honest and unselfish as I am, you will not mind my saying you are not ready for the Blue Bird."

Before Lucie had a chance to reply Piers' voice cut across the room. "Aren't you taking too much on yourself, Adana? If Jack thinks Lucie is good enough I don't see what concern it is of yours."

The ballerina wheeled round on him. "Then why are *you* so concerned?"

"I'm not. That's why I think you're making a mountain out of a molehill. As a rule you don't even notice how the other solo work is performed. Why bother now? Come and have some coffee with me and forget it."

He held out his hand and after a moment's hesitation she went to him, her face wreathed in smiles. "A good idea, Piers! Perhaps we have been working too hard, yes?"

As the door shut behind them chatter broke out amongst the company and Lucie sat down to untie her ballet shoes, wondering miserably if Adana was right and all her months of hard work had gone for nothing. And yet the ballerina had never before concerned herself with the general standard of performance – indeed there was a saying in the company that if Dennison put a horse on the stage with her she would not care as long as it did not interfere with her own work. Usually she preferred inferior dancers to support her, since it threw her own performance into sharper relief, and that she should now interest herself in one of the subsidiary dancers made Lucie suspect some underlying motive. Could it be because of Piers? It was common knowledge that the ballerina was attracted to him, and she probably resented the long hours he spent with Lucie. But why should she stop working with him to satisfy the whim of an egocentric virago? If Adana was jealous, let her prevail on Piers herself not to devote so much time to the potential Blue Bird.

But apart from a single wry remark Piers made no mention of the ballerina's outburst, and they continued to work on his latest choreography. Determined to learn as much from him as she could before Adana did anything to dissuade him, Lucie drove herself so hard that after a particularly long and strenuous practice one evening, Piers remonstrated with her.

"You can't set the world on fire in a minute, Lucie. I've told you before that double the work won't make you better in half the time."

She looked round the large, empty room, the far corners already receding as the swift dusk deepened. "It seems a pity not to make full use of this space while we can."

"There are practice-rooms all over the world," he said drily. "Or do you feel particularly inspired by the elegant piano?"

"It may be that," she smiled. "Or because I want to take advantage of you while I can."

He looked at her quizzically. "I know you don't mean that in the colloquial sense, but if you mean it literally, there's no hurry. I'll be here as long as you want me."

"Will you, Piers?"

"Of course. Did you think Adana would persuade me not to work with you?"

"Perhaps." She walked over to the barre. "You've helped me a great deal, Piers, but I – I don't want to come between you and – anything else."

"Anything else is rather a quaint way of describing it! Stop jerking about like a tee-to-tum for a moment and look at me." He moved over and cupped her head between his hands. "Don't be scared of Adana, Lucie, you've no reason to be. Since we first started working together no other woman has held any attraction for me."

"You might change your mind," she said lightly.

"I doubt it. I'm in love with you. Surely you know that?" His hands dropped abruptly and he walked back to the piano. "There, I've said it. Without any pretence or hedging I've told you how I feel. I didn't mean to yet – I was going to take you out to dinner and put you in the mood with romantic music and champagne." He looked around the darkening room. "This isn't the ideal place for a declaration of love, although I suppose it's appropriate. After all, we've spent most of our time working together and it's somehow right to tell you I love you in a practice-room."

He began to strum idly on the keys, as if dismissing the subject, but she went up behind him and covered his hands with her own.

"Piers, I didn't know – I never thought.... Is that why you've been taking all this trouble with me?"

With a suddenness that startled her he crashed his hands down in a violent discord. "No love on earth could make me think a dancer was good if she wasn't! Even if I loathed the sight of you I'd still teach you everything I knew if I thought you had talent, but that wouldn't make me love you! Do you really think I've only been working with you because I want you?"

"I didn't –"

"It has nothing to do with your dancing," he went on vehemently. "If I hadn't loved you – if you were repulsive to me – I'd still have worked with you, because I believe in you! Don't confuse my love for you as a person with my opinion of you as a dancer."

"I'm glad you said that. The other day I thought Adana might have been right about my work."

"Lucie, Lucie, if you haven't got faith in yourself, how do you expect anyone else to have it? If you're uncertain, that uncertainty will show in your work. Lack of confidence is one of your greatest drawbacks."

"I haven't had much chance of gaining any," she said ruefully. "And what little I did have was knocked out of me by my marriage."

"Oh, my darling, I'll give it back to you if you'll let me! Have you forgotten I've just told you I love you?"

"Perhaps you do now, but – "

"If you're going to say I'll get over it you'd better save your breath. I've loved you long enough to know it's the real thing. Or don't you believe me because I haven't tried to make love to you?" He caught her hands. "It hasn't been easy, you know, I'm not a robot."

"I never thought you were." Then, with an apologetic smile: "Your love affairs have been too frequent for that!"

"Many men have affairs, Lucie, and if that had been all I wanted from you I'd have tried to catch you on the rebound. I've watched you eat your heart out for your husband and I know it isn't only because of Amanda that you're so determined to succeed, but that hasn't stopped me wanting you. I can't offer you all the things your fine Julian did – I haven't a lovely home or security and background. But I can give you understanding and freedom to work because I'd be part of it. Darling, if you'd only marry me when you're free we could have a wonderful life together."

"I wish I could! But I don't love you."

"If we were married you'd grow to love me."

"It's not as easy as that. Things don't always work out the way you want them to. I know we'd make a wonderful team, but one can't just marry for ambition."

"Some people can."

"If I were that sort of person you wouldn't want me." She moved to the door. "I'm sorry I can't say what you want to hear, Piers. Perhaps it might be better if we didn't go on working together."

In three strides he was across the room. "If you say that again you'll make me wish I'd never told you I love you! I meant it when I said that dancing and love have nothing to do with each other. Forget everything I've said, and when you see me tomorrow try and pretend this conversation never took place."

"Very well." She laid a hand on his arm. "I wish I loved you, Piers. It would make life so much simpler."

"Don't worry about it, darling. Perhaps in a year or two

you'll wake up to what you're missing!" He bent and kissed her lips, a touch so fleeting that she scarcely felt it. "Now run along to bed. You've had a tiring day and it's late."

The door shut behind her and he resumed his seat at the piano, his face brooding and sad. The melancholy murmur of the sea drifted in through the open window and darkness descended on the ivory keys. With a sigh half of exasperation, half of fatigue, he stood up, banged down the lid and walked out.

CHAPTER VIII

WHEN Julian walked out of the room after his scene with Lucie he waited until he heard her drive away before he ventured downstairs. He had hardly crossed the drawing-room threshold before his mother guessed that something was amiss.

"What's the matter, Julian?"

"Nothing, Mother." He accepted a cup of tea. "You know Lucie's been here?"

"So Nurse told me. I was hoping you'd be out when she came – it can only bring back unhappy memories to see her."

"On the contrary, I'm glad I was here. If I hadn't, I might still be harbouring the illusion that we could have made a go of our marriage."

Mrs. Summerford sniffed. "I didn't think you had any illusions left where Lucie was concerned. After all she's done, you'd be foolish not to put her completely out of your mind."

"If I ever doubted it I've had proof today." He looked down at the carpet. "She came here with Bellamy."

For a moment Mrs. Summerford was nonplussed. "Do you mean she had the effrontery to bring him here?"

"Yes. They were in the nursery together." He went to the window and looked out unseeingly over the lawns. "I lost my temper and told her that in future she must come down to see Amanda on her own."

"Quite right too – I'm surprised you didn't throw him out of the house! What audacity to bring him here! The more I hear about Lucie the more incredible it is that you could have fallen in love with her. If you wanted her so much, Julian, surely there was no need to have married her."

He wheeled round. "Good lord, Mother, I never thought I'd hear you say a thing like that!"

A flush rose into the smooth cheeks. "I may be old-fashioned, Julian, but I know what goes on in the world. The only difference is that today it's talked about openly and not behind closed doors, as it was when I was a girl. Do you think I don't know that young men have affairs? I know I always said you shouldn't marry until you'd made a success of your career, but it was no concern of mine how you chose to amuse yourself. That you'd want to marry one of your amusements never occurred to me."

"Lucie was never one of my amusements," he said sharply. "She's not that kind of person."

"Her behaviour at the moment makes that hard to believe. Are you sure you weren't fooled, Julian? Men in love so often are."

"Mother, don't!"

"Very well. But I must say it was singularly bad taste to bring that man down here with her. One would have thought she'd have appreciated being alone with her child. Still, she was always rather theatrical and she probably didn't mind an audience. Next time she comes she'll have me to deal with."

"I don't think she'll be here for some time. The company's going to America quite soon."

"Really? I didn't think they were well-known enough."

Against his will he had to smile. "Just because you don't like Lucie doesn't mean the company's no good! It happens to be one of the best in the country."

"More's the pity. She's brought you so much unhappiness you can't blame me for disliking anything connected with her."

"I don't." He leaned over and touched her cheek. "While we're on the subject of Lucie I'd like to thank you for never saying 'I told you so'. Not many women would have had your forbearance."

She caught his hand. "And I've been so afraid you were blaming me for what happened."

"Blaming you? Why, if it hadn't been for you my marriage would have gone on the rocks long ago."

"You don't know what a relief it is to hear you say that." Mrs. Summerford blew her nose and put her handkerchief away with a little gesture of finality. "Now tell me everything that's been happening in London. How much longer do you expect to remain there, or don't you know yet?"

Julian lit a cigarette. "Another month at the very most. Sir John dropped a hint that I might be going fairly soon."

"Any idea where?"

"Probably the Argentine and then America."

"America?"

He looked up. "Don't worry, it's pure coincidence that Lucie'll be there at the same time."

"Well, I only hope you don't run into her. It's bad enough thinking you might meet in London." She sighed. "I'm going to be lonely without you, Julian, especially at weekends. I've got used to having you home."

"Never mind, darling, there's Amanda."

"She's no compensation for you. Still, as long as you're making progress I'll try not to mind. Perhaps when you're an Ambassador I'll come along and be your hostess!"

"You'd love that, wouldn't you? Then you'd really have a chance to boast about all the virtues I haven't got!"

"I'm not unique in being vain about my son – most mothers are, and for far less reason."

"You're a mother in a million," he said fondly.

"And you're a son who deserves it!"

But although they had dismissed Lucie from their conversation, Julian found it impossible to dismiss her from his thoughts. Always in the back of his mind had lain the hope that one day they would come together again; her arrival at Combe House with Bellamy had shown him how far they had drifted apart. Had he been wrong to accuse her of being Piers' mistress? When she had left him she had gone to Piers, when she had started work again it had been with him; she had even brought him down to see the baby. And yet, and yet . . .

During his remaining weekends in Devon Julian spent as much time as he could with Amanda. Since the day Lucie had put her in his arms he began to find a world of pleasure in his little daughter, and delighted in watching the play of expression on her face and the development of intelligence in the dark grey eyes. As her face took on character her likeness to Lucie grew more pronounced, and although the memories she roused were bitter-sweet he continued to pay long visits to the nursery, unwilling to admit even to himself that it was the only place where he did not have to hide his loneliness from solicitous eyes.

His last weekend in Devon before his departure for South America, Julian drove over to see Ann and Francis. It was the first time he had spoken to his sister-in-law since his accident, and although no mention was made of Lucie, Ann brought her so vividly to mind that he left Mayfields with a feeling of relief.

Francis rode with him to the end of the lane and cheerily wished him god-speed. "Don't forget to write from them thar furrin parts," he grinned.

"I won't. And you keep me posted how things are going on the estate and how Mother's keeping. Don't let her get too lonely while I'm away."

Francis clambered out of the car. "If only Ann would be sensible and move back to Combe House. It's ridiculous for Mother to live in such a big place on her own."

"It's even more ridiculous to think of moving back. Ann's too quick-tempered to live in the same house with another woman. Besides, Mother's had enough to put up with these last few months without any more disagreements. It'll be better if you keep your womenfolk apart."

"That's easier said than done. When I leave Mother to go home she's upset and when I walk out of Mayfields Ann looks like thunder." Francis grimaced. "Oh well, something'll happen one of these days, I suppose. Domestic crises usually sort themselves out in the end." He gripped his brother's hand. "Look after yourself, old chap."

"Thanks. You do the same."

Mrs. Summerford saw Julian go with tears in her eyes. If it had not been for Amanda she might have persuaded him to take her with him. Why had Lucie had to have a child? Without the little girl there would have been no reminder of her son's unfortunate marriage, no evidence that he had ever fallen in love and brought a stranger into her home.

Never in all the months since the marriage had failed had she felt a pang of self-reproach for hastening its failure. If Lucie suffered, what of it? She was still young enough to make a new life for herself. No woman would ever be able to take away her sons.

Francis' marriage had been a severe blow, for any hope she had had of ruling his wife had been dispelled by Ann's own force of character. It was in Francis' nature to steer an ineffectual course between his wife and his mother, his vacillating temperament leading him to take the line of least resistance.

But with Julian it was different. A sensitive man like his father, of the same high integrity, he blindly followed his oldest loyalty. For him there was no middle way, no compromise or policy of arbitration, and this unswerving devotion had made it easier to part him from Lucie. She refused to face the possibility that he might marry again one day. Suffice that he was free now – or would be, as soon as he could obtain a divorce. For the time being matters had been taken out of her hands by his posting abroad.

Contrary to his expectations, Julian thoroughly enjoyed his six months in Buenos Aires. His work was interesting, the social life was full and amusing, and the women exceptionally lovely. It would have been easy to become involved in an affair, and although there were times when he was tempted by the questioning of dark eyes or stirred by the touch of a soft hand, a determination not to repeat past folly held him back.

Now that he was away from England and so many miles away from Lucie he was able to think more objectively about their marriage. He had loved her so much once, and such a short time ago, that it was hard to believe he would never hold her in his arms again. Had he treated her too much like a child – was that why she had gone to another man? And yet in Paris during the first few months of their life together, there had been no restraint, no false reticence, and she had responded to him with a depth of love equally his own. If only she had given him time to find his feet, what a heaven-sent opportunity these months in Buenos Aires would have been!

If his broken marriage had done nothing else it had given him greater resilence, and the hard-won maturity he was beginning to gain stood him in good stead throughout the long and difficult negotiations with which he had to deal. His work did not go unnoticed in London, and Sir John Ranken wrote and congratulated him, expressing the hope that he would have similar success in America.

Julian left the white city of Buenos Aires with regret and flew north across the Amazon, snatching a week's respite in Jamaica before he proceeded to Washington.

The tempo of life in the capital was vastly different from that of the South American city; here the day's work was done with a vigorous intensity that precluded any waste of time on the mere elegance is of professional intercourse. But once the business of the day was done Julian found that the Americans, like no other people, knew how to enjoy themselves, and soon became ruefully aware from his own fatigue that they played as hard as they worked.

A topic on everyone's lips was the Dennison Ballet and in particular the success of a young choreographer, Piers Bellamy. But of Lucie he heard nothing and would have given a great deal to know what was happening in her life.

CHAPTER IX

The first performance of the Dennison Ballet was warmly received in Philadelphia, the American critics welcoming it in glowing terms.

After the luxury of their sojourn in Miami the dust and heat of Philadelphia was a trying contrast, but gradually summer gave way to autumn and they were able to appreciate the splendour of Fairmont Park and the gracious beauty of one of the oldest American cities.

Piers' declaration of love had done much to restore Lucie's self-esteem, and the atmosphere between them was subtly altered. Where before she had been unaware of his physical proximity, she was now acutely conscious of his hand on her shoulder or the pressure of his arm around her waist whenever they danced together.

It was about this time that she was able to abandon herself more freely to interpretation, and Dennison watched her with an interest only tempered by the caution that experience had taught him. Piers was secretly badgering him to let Lucie dance the leading rôle in his new ballet, *The Golden Fleece*, and he might have agreed had he not been afraid of arousing Adana's fury. But to allow Lucie to take precedence over the ballerina would have been unethical as well as dangerous, and he reluctantly told Piers that Adana must be offered the rôle first.

Lucie was relieved when Adana consented to dance the part, for she did not feel confident enough to undertake it herself and secretly hoped that Piers would be too occupied with the ballerina to brood over her own rejection of his love.

But there was another side to the picture. Adana's long hours of rehearsal with Piers soon reduced her to a state of tempestuous frustration, and realising that if he tried her too far she might wreck his ballet out of pique, he had no option but to try and placate her. Had he been less in love with Lucie, Piers would have found the ballerina irresistible, but against Lucie's fragile delicacy she seemed flamboyant and over-blown. When she held up her inviting red mouth for his good night kiss it was an effort to touch it with his own, and he only did so in the hope of averting a crisis until the first performance of the new ballet was over. Once the critics had seen it he did not care what happened, but if Adana took it into her head to misinterpret the part she could do his reputation as a choreographer incalculable harm.

It was unfortunate that three days before the opening of *The Golden Fleece* Adana decided to throw discretion to the winds. Never had she wanted any man who had not wanted her, and that this young dancer with the thin, pointed face and slanting eyes should hold himself aloof was more than her vanity would allow. After the performance that night she insisted he visit her hotel suite for supper.

She welcomed him in a negligée that left little to the imagination, and walked straight over to the magnum of champagne cooling in an ice-bucket.

"Come, darling, we will draw the cork."

Over dinner Piers kept her amused with a series of anecdotes about the company, but when the meal was over it was difficult to evade the inevitable, for Adana draped herself invitingly at one end of the couch and patted the place beside her.

"Come and sit down, Piers. It is late and you are tired. You must relax, dear."

He yawned prodigiously. "Yes, I'm damned tired. Perhaps I'd better be going."

"Silly boy, you need not go so soon. Sit down and forget about everything." She patted the couch again, but he refused to take the hint. "Darling Piers, there's no need to be afraid of me. Why are you so nervous? I won't bite!" She held up her hand imperiously her temper wearing as thin as the chiffon covering her breast. "Don't be so unkind to me, Piers. It isn't nice to tease me like this. We could be so happy, if you would be less cold. Don't you think I'm beautiful?"

"Of course I do, but surely you don't need me to tell you?"

"You are the only one I want to tell it to me! All the others are nothing."

Hearing her mouth words he had so often used gave Piers the feeling that he was watching a parody of himself.

"I am waiting," came the soft, insidious voice. "Do you not want to kiss me?"

Seeing no way to refuse, he lightly touched her mouth with his own, but as he drew back she pulled him against her. Subtle dancer she might be, but in love her only axiom was to take what she wanted, and she offered herself to him blatantly, abandonment in every line of her body.

Tearing off her clinging arms and forcing himself away from the greedy mouth, Piers threw her back against the cushions and stood up. She regarded him for an instant from beneath lowered lids, then realising that his withdrawal was no pretence but genuine recoil, an ugly flush mounted into her cheeks.

"You are not going to leave me, Piers?"

"That's exactly what I am going to do." Regardless now of whether he angered her or not, only knowing that unless he left this languorous, heavily perfumed woman he would be unable to hide his revulsion, he moved to the door.

In a blaze of silken fury Adana barred his way. "How dare you insult me like this?" she screamed. "I want you, and what I want I have!"

"I'm afraid you can't this time."

"Be careful what you say, Piers! It is dangerous to drive me too far." The stridency of her voice dropped abruptly and she rested her body against him. "Don't go away, dear, we were made for each other. I love you Piers – I want you!"

"Damn it, Adana, I don't want *you* and I never have – is that plain enough?"

She drew back with a hissing sound and pulled her negligée close around her, the picture of affronted virginity. "No man has ever said that to me before! Don't try me too far or I will never forgive you."

"That wouldn't worry me."

"Wouldn't it?" she shrilled. "We'll see about that. It is because of Lucie, isn't it? Everywhere I go this pale-faced baby is before me!" Her rage mounted. "Morning, noon and night you're dancing with her; everywhere I go I see you together. It's too much. I'll kill her, I tell you, I'll kill her!"

"Shut up, you little hell-cat!"

He put his hand across her mouth, but she tore it away, leaving red weals on its back. "I will not be quiet! How dare you defend a nobody against me – me, Adana! She should have stayed with her husband where she belongs – in the kitchen!

That's all she's good for – to wash dishes!"

With an exclamation he turned away.

"Piers!" she shrieked, "if you leave me, I leave your ballet!"

He looked at her in silence. Then with a shrug he opened the door and walked out.

Returning to his hotel Piers could scarcely believe that the scene he had been dreading so long had finally taken place. If Adana had refused the part a month ago, how much simpler everything would have been! But to do so now, when the first performance was only three days away, set him an almost insoluble problem. Ever since he had conceived the ballet, it had been his ambition for Lucie to dance Medea, but to expect her to take on the rôle at such short notice might do her irreparable harm. Better to shelve the ballet altogether for the time being.

Lucie, however, would not hear of it. "You can't postpone it, Piers! If you do, Dennison might never give you another chance of putting it on. Are you sure Adana won't change her mind?"

"Not unless I change mine, and I couldn't make love to a woman I loathe!"

"Then there's nothing for it but for me to take over the part."

"I don't want to put you on if you're not ready – it wouldn't be fair to you."

"You once said that confidence is one of the most important things in a dancer's life, and the one part I feel confident of is Medea. If you'll let me, Piers, I'd like to do it."

He hugged her convulsively. "I was hoping you'd say that, darling! Thank heavens you did."

The next three days passed in a maelstrom of activity. When they were not rehearsing with the company Lucie and Piers worked together, stopping to argue and discuss, but always dancing, dancing, dancing. At night Lucie was so tired she could hardly sleep; every muscle ached, every tendon nagged, but she would get up next morning and uncomplainingly repeat what she had done the day before.

A few hours before the curtain was due to go up Dennison was padding round the empty stage like a caged bear, Piers was taut with suspense and every member of the company except Adana was strung to breaking point. Lucie had not left the theatre all day and looked so wan that Piers insisted she rest in her dressing-room. Although she obeyed his instructions and lay down on the couch her mind was too full of the coming performance to sleep, and she lay with closed eyes, going through one scene after another.

At last the auditorium began to fill and as the sound of the orchestra tuning up floated through the bare corridors she bent forward to lace her pumps. Her costume of rose chiffon fell in classical folds, the loose ends of material floating diaphanously as she moved to the mirror and drew her hair into a Grecian knot, attaching the bunch of artificial curls that sprang from it. All too soon the call-boy with the American accent knocked on the door and announced that the curtain was rising, and accepting her dresser's good wishes with a tight smile, she left the room.

Lucie remembered little of her performance that night. From the moment she stepped on to the stage her whole being was focussed on the arduous rôle of Medea, for whose love Jason was to undertake his perilous quest. Piers did everything he could to make her ordeal easier, guiding her through the most difficult passages and intricate movements, his strong arms supporting her in the repeated lifts, staunchly at her side when she executed her pirouettes and fouettés. When the final curtain descended to a thunder of applause she turned to him with tears in her eyes and kissed him before they went forward to take their call.

There were fifteen curtain calls, fifteen vociferous rounds of applause, and it was not until the stage lights were dimmed that the audience stopped clapping and began to file out.

The minute Lucie stepped into the wings she was greeted by Dennison and Madame Molina.

"Tonight you danced as I've never seen you dance before," Jack Dennison beamed. "It was hard to forgive you for leaving us, but after such a performance I can forget anything. Perhaps we can have a little celebration?"

"I think Lucie would prefer to have dinner à deux," Madame Molina's fat face creased into a knowing smile.

"If you say so." Dennison accepted the refusal gracefully. "Come and see me tomorrow, Lucie, there are several things to discuss. We must put your name on the bill and see about letting you share some of Adana's rôles."

Piers made a face. "I don't envy you having to tell her. It'll be a bitter pill for her to swallow Lucie's success at all."

"That's not my fault," Dennison growled. "In work I know only of dancers – and the best must lead. If we're lucky enough to have two prima ballerinas in our company I will not sacrifice one to the jealousy of the other." He patted Piers' shoulder. "I'm as pleased with you as I am with Lucie – you'll go a long way. The ballet is good – even better than I expected." He turned to the ballet mistress. "Come along, I can see we're not wanted here."

He lumbered across the stage towards the prompt corner, and Lucie put her arm through Piers'.

"It's enough to take your breath away!" she said excitedly. "For years you're in the corps and suddenly you're a ballerina!"

"Not so suddenly," he replied. "You've worked damn hard for it."

"One's always ready to forget what one doesn't want to remember!"

"I hope that remark doesn't include me? After all, you associate me with the hard grind and criticism."

She hugged his arm. "I owe my success to you, Piers darling."

"Rubbish, you owe it to yourself! Now run and change and I'll meet you at the stage door. We'll have supper together."

There began for Lucie an entirely new phase in her life. To their surprise Dennison's bland assumption that Adana would accept the change in Lucie's status was justified, for after a display of tantrums exceeding all others she settled down to the new arrangement, too astute to jeopardise her own position by refusing to co-operate.

The critics had received them with unstinted delight, but this was still Philadelphia. How would they be reviewed in New York, that sternest of cities, where artists accepted in other countries were so often rejected?

They had no need to worry. Every critic of note received them with praise, and after the first night they played to capacity houses. They were booked at one of the smaller theatres, but at the end of their run were transferred to a larger theatre on Broadway where they went from success to success.

It was Lucie who attracted most attention, and with a sureness built on steady progress she came to the notice of the New York audiences, who returned again and again to see her, quick to recognise that here was an artist of rare lyrical beauty and technique. "She floats across the stage like thistledown blown by a summer breeze" – one rhapsodist allowed his pen to run away with him – "and on her delightful shoulders rests the failure or success of *The Golden Fleece*."

As autumn gave way to winter and the trees in Central Park turned brown and shed their leaves, Lucie's dancing subtly altered and she began to experience the full freedom of artistic control.

To Piers she was an unfailing source of satisfaction, and watching her from the stalls during rehearsals or from the wings while they were performing, he experienced the pride of a creator. He refused to think of the future. Enough to accept the present without tormenting himself how long it would last.

Looking out of her hotel bedroom at the lights of the city one evening, Lucie suddenly thought of Julian. It seemed a lifetime since he had told her he might be sent here. On an impulse she picked up her handbag and re-read the latest letter from Blackmer giving news of Amanda.

"Your little girl is quite well," he wrote, "and I am told she is learning to walk and talk and has grown considerably." How cold and formal it was – "she is learning to walk and talk." Yet to Lucie it meant all she was missing of Amanda's development: the soft babble giving way to the experimental sounds of early speech, the ungainly crawl emerging into the first tottering steps – this was something she would never see, something no trick of time could ever recapture, and she felt cheated of a happiness that was her right.

A few streets away Julian was reading of the arrival of the Dennison Ballet. Returning to his hotel to change for dinner, his glance had immediately fallen on the numerous photographs of the dancers, amazed to see Lucie's looking back at him over the caption: "Lucinda Marlow, a ballerina Washington is waiting to see." At first he could scarcely believe it was the same Lucie. How svelte she looked, how poised and well-groomed! He studied the small, heart-shaped face, the candid eyes looking out at him with the expression he remembered so well, and his mind was filled with memories.

During the next week he could not pick up a paper without reading her name. "Marlow first night." "Marlow's brilliant rendition of Aurora." "Marlow's Swanhilda excels." Everyone he spoke to seemed to have heard about her or seen her, and he wondered what his colleagues at the Embassy would think if they knew that Julian Summerford, the correct Englishman, was married to this glamorous dancer.

In a country where Combe House seemed unreal, he was sufficiently free from the trammels of his upbringing to analyse much that he had shut out of his mind before, and his belief that Lucie and Bellamy were lovers had faltered. Away from his mother's influence he was able to look back on Lucie's behaviour with greater perception, and although far from willing to admit she had been justified in running away he conceded that she had had extreme provocation to do so. He knew he must make a decision about his marriage one way or the other and he could not go back to England without first seeing Lucie.

The British Ambassador took the decision out of his hands by arranging a reception for the Dennison company in appreciation of the prestige they had achieved for British ballet in America. All the senior staff of the Embassy were to attend the performance beforehand, and Julian had no option but to go – indeed, it was a heaven-sent opportunity to meet Lucie without taking the initiative himself.

The Embassy staff occupied two boxes near the stage, and in the absence of her husband on some last-minute official business, the Ambassador's wife insisted on Julian sitting next to her.

"We'll soon be losing you and it may be some time before we meet. In any case, I hope you'll remember me to your mother. I met her several times through Lady Ranken."

His mother! What would she think if she knew he was sitting in a Washington theatre waiting to see Lucie dance? His train of thought was interrupted by the auditorium lights being dimmed, the conductor took the stand to a round of applause, and a sweep of violins heralded the rising of the curtain. The first half of the programme was devoted to a modern ballet, but Julian's mind was too full of the prospect of seeing

Lucie to concentrate and he waited impatiently for the second half when she was to appear in "Daphnis and Chloe."

The curtain rose after the interval to reveal the entrance to the cave of Pan, and he leaned forward in his seat. The corps de ballet came on, worshippers bearing their gifts of flowers and fruit, and then, almost lost in the throng of dancers, the slight figures of a man and a girl made their entrance, to be greeted by a burst of applause.

Julian picked up his opera glasses. The man was Bellamy and the girl Lucie, a lovely figure in a pleated yellow tunic, her hair caught into ringlets which bounced and bobbed as she pirouetted joyously amongst the crowd. A roll of drums heralded the approach of pirates and the villagers fled, leaving the stage empty except for the lovers, who were too engrossed in each other to be aware of danger until they were surrounded and Chloe was carried off, leaving Daphnis prostrate by the sea-shore as the curtain descended on the first scene.

Almost before the applause died down the curtains parted again to reveal the pirates taunting their fragile captive. Desperately Chloe tried to escape, but she was tossed from one man to another, until at last, defenceless and exhausted, she fell fainting in the centre of the stage.

Suddenly the tempo of the music changed and the god Pan appeared and loosened Chloe's chains. Terror-stricken the pirates fled, and the scene reverted once more to the sea-shore where Daphnis still lay bemoaning his loss. A lightening of the stage foretold the approach of dawn as Chloe came ashore from a small boat, and there followed the most beautiful love duet Julian had ever seen. Here were dancers of the most consummate skill. Holding Lucie in his arms, lifting her, leaping, pirouetting, Piers personified a lover entirely enmeshed in his passion. The music undulated as he rocked her to and fro, evoking the very spirit of desire without crudity or overstatement, and when at last the curtain descended there was a moment of complete silence before the deafening applause began.

Julian found himself clapping until his hands were tired, clapping until the curtain had descended leaving him with a vision of Lucie smiling at Piers over an enormous bouquet.

With an effort he returned to earth. "Wasn't it wonderful?" the Ambassador's wife was saying. "What an exquisite creature Lucie Marlow is!"

"Exquisite," he echoed.

During the reception Julian tried to hide his fever of anticipation as he chatted with one group of people and another. "Yes, the performance was wonderful.... We're proud British ballet has been such a success over here.... I quite agree, it's an international language, about the only one left..." Talking, talking, and always about the ballet; making the appropriate remarks, however platitudinous, while his eyes continually strayed towards the door and his mind was full of Lucie. He was reminded of the time he had gone backstage after he had first seen her dance the Blue Bird. How colourless she had seemed then without her costume or make-up! Would that same difference strike him now?

But the party had been in full swing for some time before the Ambassador went forward to greet Jack Dennison and the principal dancers. Julian was standing at the bar with a South American diplomat he had known in Buenos Aires and his eyes travelled quickly over the group until he found Lucie, the hand in which he held his cigarette shaking as he raised it to his lips. Never had he seen her look lovelier or more sophisticated. Her perfectly plain black dress was caught at the waist with a wide topaz-studded belt almost the colour of her hair, which was drawn back into a sleek halo, and every time she moved her head topaz ear-rings caught the light. Bellamy was at her side as they moved down the room, greeting and being greeted, and Julian wondered apprehensively what her reaction would be when she saw him.

Lucie accepted a glass of champagne and talked to the Ambassador and his wife, gratified to find them extremely knowledgeable about the ballet. Piers was in earnest conversation with a dapper, bearded foreigner, Dennison and Madame Molina were busily consuming sandwiches and conversing volubly with a group of distinguished balletomanes, and when her host and hostess were called away to greet a late arrival Lucie found herself temporarily alone. Realising she was ravenously hungry she moved towards the buffet, accepting another glass of champagne from a passing waiter as she did so.

"I wouldn't drink that on an empty stomach if I were you," someone said at her elbow.

She did not need to look round to know that the voice was Julian's. In her first quick glance she saw that the past months had changed him little; his dark eyes were just as intense, his voice as quick and low. With a helpless pang she knew he had lost none of his attraction for her.

"Hullo, Julian, I didn't know you were here. How are you?"

"Very well, thanks. I needn't ask how you are – you look radiant."

She accepted the compliment with an ease unfamiliar to him. "Thank you. You look very well yourself."

He smiled. "Even if the champagne hasn't gone to your head I'm sure you'd like to sit down. You must be tired after your performance."

Still the same solicitous courtesy – if only there were some depth behind his good manners! But she followed him to an alcove and sat down without any sign of the turmoil she felt at meeting him again.

He held out his cigarette case and then drew it back. "I was forgetting – you don't smoke."

"That's something that hasn't changed since we last saw each other."

"I suppose a good many other things have?"

"Time doesn't stand still." Then with a sudden change of tone: "Julian, how's Amanda? I hardly ever hear about her. Is she well? Does she walk properly yet? Can she talk?"

"I've got some photographs in my wallet if you'd like to see them."

"Oh, I would!" Eagerly she took the snapshots from his hand and studied them intently, and watching the downbent head with its cameo profile, the short upper lip and the soft down at her temples, Julian wanted desperately to take her in his arms.

"How she's grown!" Lucie exclaimed, and looking up, caught the expression on his face. "What's the matter, Julian?"

"Nothing. I – it's just the shock of seeing you again."

"That doesn't sound very complimentary."

"I'm sorry, I meant it as one. You've come a long way since you left me, Lucie. I'm glad you made such a success of your career. It was what you wanted, wasn't it?"

"Not in the first place – but I had no choice." She put a hand to her hair in a gesture he knew well. "I either had to leave you or be suffocated at Combe House. The ballet was the only thing I could go back to. But you've come a long way too. I believe you're quite a diplomat these days."

"Perhaps if I'd been as diplomatic in my private life as I have to be in my job I might not be sitting here talking to you like a stranger," he said with sudden bitterness.

She handed him back the photographs, but he pushed them into her lap again and she accepted the gift with a slight smile. "Life is full of ifs and buts, Julian. They're little words that can mean an awful lot."

"You still haven't answered me."

"About what?"

"That if I'd been more diplomatic we wouldn't be sitting here like strangers."

She pondered for a moment. "I wonder if you really think that, or whether you're just saying it? Are you trying to tell me you've realised I was right?"

"Right?"

A tight smile flitted across her face. "Ah, you've answered me without meaning to! If you'd really understood the question you'd have known the answer without having to ask."

"I don't see how you can expect me to admit you were right. After all, you walked out on me." He leant forward. "Oh, Lucie, why were you so impatient – couldn't you have waited a bit longer?"

"Waited for what? To be more disillusioned by you and frustrated by your mother? I didn't want to break up our marriage, Julian. When I went to London I did it to try and jerk you into some sort of independence and responsibility towards me and Amanda, and for weeks I hoped you'd follow. You can't blame me if you took the easy way out."

"Damn it, Lucie, when I did come you were with Bellamy!"

"And you naturally jumped to the wrong conclusions, insinuated no doubt by your mother."

He flinched. "Time hasn't softened your tongue."

"It was sharpened during my marriage. I had to use it in self-defence, and my life since hasn't done anything to soften it."

"But you're very successful."

"Now, yes. But success didn't drop into my lap, and whether you believe it or not, I didn't leave you for the sake of my career. Now, of course, it means a great deal."

"And Amanda and I – don't we mean anything to you?"

"Really, Julian, it's stupid to ask a question like that."

He stood up. "We can't talk properly here. Let's go out on the terrace."

"I can't –"

"Please," he insisted. "I won't keep you long."

They threaded their way through the crowded room to the paved terrace overlooking the Embassy lawns.

Lucie shivered. "I should have brought my wrap."

"I'm sorry," he said abruptly, "I forgot you never dressed warmly enough, but we won't be out here long." He propelled her to a sheltered spot and took up a stance in front of her. "Now then, why am I stupid? Forgive me if I still don't know."

"Because it's ridiculous to ask if Amanda means anything to me. The only reason I've worked is to be able to fight for her. I didn't leave you because I'd stopped loving you but because I couldn't stand by and watch you being dominated by someone else. I wanted a home of my own, and I thought I'd get it more quickly if I ran away. When you came to find me it was merely to take Amanda."

"But I thought you'd gone to Piers."

"He was my only friend," she said simply, "and the one person who could help me get a job."

"If it was as simple as that I've been a damn fool, but you can't blame me for thinking what I did, and you certainly can't blame Mother. She had our best interests at heart."

"Do you really believe that, Julian, in spite of everything that's happened?"

"Of course. But I admit I was to blame for not seeing that you two were incompatible."

"At least you realise that." She shivered again and instinctively he put out his arms to protect her, dropping them awkwardly a second after he had made the gesture.

"No, it's not fair to hold you. I want to be able to talk clearly, and I can't do that if you're in my arms. Lucie, I love you and I want you to come back to me. I'm not asking you to give up your career, you've come too far for that. All I ask is for you to come back to me and Amanda."

She turned away convulsively. "Julian, I can't! You don't understand. You would never give our marriage a chance. And even if you would, your mother would soon put a stop to that."

He flushed. "Why do you have to keep dragging Mother into it?"

"Because – oh, Julian, can't you see? As long as you refuse to see what your mother's doing there's no hope for us. There's nothing more to be said."

Blinking back her tears, Lucie walked ahead of him into the crowded room, but before she could reach the door Piers was at her side.

"I was just coming to find you – where have you been?" He caught sight of Julian and his expression tightened. "I didn't know you were here, Summerford. Come along, Lucie, it's late, we must go."

Lucie was not conscious of saying good-bye to her host and hostess, and even when they reached the hotel she moved and spoke like an automaton.

"Snap out of it, Lucie," Piers said lightly. "It's only to be expected that you're upset at seeing Julian again."

She made an effort to smile. "It wasn't that so much as the memories he brought back. Perhaps if I'd known he was going to be there. . . ."

"Surely it wasn't so catastrophic? Meetings like that must happen to hundreds of people in similar positions. Come, darling, buck up, or I'll think you're still in love with him."

"Don't be ridiculous," she said sharply. "Just because I'm a little upset –"

"He asked you to go back to him, didn't he?" Piers interrupted.

For the first time Lucie looked fully into his face. "Yes. But I'm not going to. I can't fight his mother, and he won't."

CHAPTER X

It would have been little consolation if Lucie had known how deeply Julian was hurt. Once the first shock had worn off he touched the lowest ebb of desolation, at one moment blaming himself, at the next filled with angry condemnation of what he still obstinately thought of as Lucie's intolerance of his mother.

Amanda had grown amazingly in his absence, and was such a forcible reminder of the woman he wanted to forget that after the first few days at home he did not visit the nursery, and occupied himself with the estate. For the first time he was struck with Francis' continual presence in the house – not a day passed without his brother being there – and although Julian was glad of the companionship he wondered whether Francis ever spent an evening with his wife.

The days at home dragged; never before had he counted the hours and looked so often at his watch. Why was it that everyone seemed to have changed? Had his mother always asked him where he was going whenever he left the house? Had she always wanted to know what he was thinking when he was silent? Even Simon was no longer the same. Gone was the usual cheerful vitality and instead he was taciturn and short-tempered.

Perhaps because of the very monotony Julian decided to see Ann again, and late one afternoon he drove over to Mayfields.

His sister-in-law was upstairs when he pushed open the front door, but the minute he called she came running down. "Hullo, stranger!"

"Hullo, Ann." Unexpectedly he kissed her. "How are you?"

"Not too bad. How are you?"

She led him into the lounge and they sat down on the sofa in front of the empty grate. It was warm for early spring and the windows were open to the soft breeze that blew the cretonne curtains into the room.

She appraised him. "You look as if a rest would do you good. Did you enjoy America or were you too busy working?"

"I did work pretty hard, but I'm on a month's leave now –

that should do the trick. You're looking tired too." There were lines around her eyes he had not noticed before, and he did not like the quick gestures with which she accompanied her remarks.

"I *am* tired, Julian." She stood up and walked jerkily around the room. "Tired of pretending my marriage is worth saving, tired of trying not to let the children see how far apart Francis and I have drifted. So tired that I don't think I can go on any longer."

Her outburst was so sudden that he realised she was strung almost to breaking point.

"Surely it isn't as bad as that, old girl?" he said uneasily. "Why not get Francis to take you away for a while?"

She snorted. "Don't *you* start pretending, Julian! Haven't you had enough of it, or are you too well-bred to see what's under your nose? Francis and I are finished! I've known it for a long time, but now I must do something about it."

"I didn't realise. . . . Forgive me."

She took a cigarette from the box on the mantelpiece and lit it before she spoke again. "I think I might have gone on like this for the rest of my life if it hadn't been for Lucie. But when she had the courage to clear out and make a new life for herself I started to face facts."

"You don't intend to follow her example, do you?" He was shocked. "Think of the children!"

"They're all I've thought of for the last seven years! I'm still a young woman, Julian, and I want some happiness out of life. If I left Francis my parents would gladly look after the boys."

"I never thought I'd hear you talk so cold-bloodedly about breaking up your home."

"Poor Julian, always expecting people to do the right thing! You don't know very much about human nature, do you?"

"Perhaps not. But there's a common basis of decency for everyone."

"And there's a common basis of intelligence in dealing with situations like this. No two people think alike about these things – your code isn't mine and mine mightn't be someone else's. I've got to do what I think will be best in the long run. You're too rigid, Julian, and if you don't mind my saying so, rather immature. You believe things because you want to believe them, without thinking for yourself. Didn't Lucie's running away have any effect on you whatever?"

"It broke up my marriage, if that's what you mean."

"But didn't it make you think more clearly? Didn't you wonder what drove her to it? Can you sit there and tell me you *still* think she's to blame?"

A flicker of uncertainty passed over his face. "I still think she took the wrong way out. You don't solve problems by running away from them."

"And you don't solve them by staying where you are! You've got to act sooner or later."

"So you think Lucie was right to leave me and Amanda?"

"Lucie *didn't* leave Amanda," Ann said quietly.

Julian gestured angrily. "All right, she took the baby with her, but to what? To a squalid kitchen in a back street! To be looked after by some slut of a landlady while she was at the theatre all day? If Lucie was content with that, I wasn't."

"But she had no intention of making it a permanent arrangement! She hoped you'd let her stay with you in London."

He rounded on her. "That's what she says now, but when I went after her she was with Bellamy."

"Not in the sense that you mean. You should have waited to see her, Julian, she was your wife and you owed it to her. You wouldn't have behaved so callously if your mother hadn't been with you."

"You're very bitter against Mother, aren't you, Ann? Like Lucie, you can't find a nice word to say about her. What harm has she ever done you? Her only fault is that she's always loved her children too much."

"That can be worse than not loving them enough."

His mouth tightened. "I think we'd better change the subject. I don't want to quarrel with you."

"And I don't want to quarrel with *you*. But it wasn't easy to stand by and see your marriage break up for the same reason as mine. Why don't you wake up before it's too late, Julian? If I left Francis tomorrow your mother wouldn't mind in the least."

"Nonsense – she'd do everything she could to make you come back!"

"Is that why she keeps Francis at Combe House all the time, knowing how much it hurts me? No, Julian, your mother parted you and Lucie and she's trying to do the same with Francis and me. She wants you both to herself and she'll probably get you in the end." She stubbed out her cigarette. "I can see you and Francis living with her for the rest of your lives, loving the woman who's destroyed your happiness because she's made you believe she's done everything for your own good."

"Really, Ann, you're letting your imagination run away with you – you must be hysterical!"

"I'm not in the least hysterical and I only wish it *was* imagination! One day when your mother isn't with you any longer you'll realise that I'm speaking the truth. I only hope that when the time comes it won't be too late for you to salvage something from the wreck she's made."

"I think I'd better go. My visit seems to have brought on one of your outbursts."

She shrugged. "Before I married your brother I was a very level-headed person."

"Possibly. At the moment you're a thoroughly neurotic woman." He went to the door. "I don't know what Mother's done to deserve two daughters-in-law like you and Lucie. You're a mother yourself, Ann, and one day you may do the very things you're blaming her for now."

"I hope I love my children less selfishly. If I ever –"

He closed the door on her and walked out. But driving home it was not so easy to shut Ann's accusations from his mind, for there had been a ring of sincerity in her voice that was anything but neurotic. It was curious that his mother should have excited such animosity in both her son's wives. She herself had not had much happiness – first her own marriage ending in the untimely death of his father, then his going on the rocks, and now Francis's. Did his brother realise what was happening? Unless he did something about it soon Francis would be as lonely as he was himself, there was that much truth in what Ann had said. And yet would his brother ever be lonely? As long as there was Combe House and his mother he would be contented enough. That was where they differed: to him Combe House was empty, the estate bare and his mother's companionship no compensation for the loss of a wife.

Lucie, Lucie! He whispered her name over and over again, filled with sudden longing for her to be sitting by his side as she had sat when he had first brought her home.

Parking his car in front of the house, he walked round into the garden and paused on the terrace to look down at Amanda on the lawn with his mother and Nurse Richards. The little girl was wearing a brief sun-suit, her fair hair pulled back from her face with a ribbon. She was singing, tunelessly to herself as she pirouetted over the grass a few yards away from her grandmother, and afraid of interrupting her, he started to walk silently across the lawn towards them.

As he did so his mother's voice rang out sharply: "Amanda, how many times have I told you not to dance? Stop it this minute!"

"But I like it, Ganma. Look, I'se a fairy!" She floated lightly towards the two women and Julian thought how winsome she looked, how like Lucie.

"Do as you're told, Amanda," Mrs. Summerford said harshly. "I won't have you disobey me!" She reached out and shook the child violently. "You're not to dance, do you hear, you're not to dance."

"Leave Amanda alone, Mother!"

At the sound of his voice Mrs. Summerford's hand dropped and with a cry the little girl ran towards him. "Daddy, Daddy, I'se frightened! Ganma says I mustn't dance!"

Julian picked Amanda up in his arms, disturbed to find her trembling. "Don't be frightened, darling, Grandma didn't mean it. Nurse Richards, take Amanda indoors."

He waited until they were out of sight before he turned to his mother. The bright sunlight mercilessly showed up every line and wrinkle, but he saw the sagging, discoloured skin without any of his usual compassion for age. For the first time he noticed the hard lines on either side of the mouth, and the heavy-lidded eyes with their bird-like sharpness, the hair as black as ever. Strange that a woman who had been through so much should still be so dark, while he . . . He ran a hand quickly over the grey at his temples.

"I don't want you to speak to Amanda like that, Mother. You're not to check her natural impulses."

"Nonsense, you've got to check children! I'm sorry it should have upset you, but you only see Amanda when she's well-behaved. Every child must learn the difference between right and wrong, and –"

"I don't happen to think dancing *is* wrong. It's a perfectly harmless outlet."

"I don't agree with you. She obviously has it in her blood and it must be curbed."

"Why? After all, Amanda's Lucie's daughter."

"Exactly." Mrs. Summerford rose and picked up her sun-glasses. "If you don't mind your child following in her mother's footsteps, there's nothing more to be said."

"If Amanda ever danced as well as her mother, I'd be proud of her."

"I never thought you'd defend Lucie after all she's done to you!"

"I'm not defending her, Mother." He was suddenly weary of the whole discussion. "I only want you to realise that as far as inheritance is concerned Amanda's Lucie's child as well as mine and to inhibit any inborn trait might do her irreparable harm."

"Modern psychological nonsense!"

"Nonsense or not, it's the way I feel."

"Very well, but don't say I didn't warn you." She began to cross the lawn. "The next thing I'll hear is that you'll want to send her to a ballet school!"

He smiled and proffered his arm. "You never know, Mother, you never know."

Harmony was soon restored between them, but now that they had crossed swords over Amanda Julian watched his mother carefully, and was gradually forced to the conclusion that she harboured an active dislike for her granddaughter. He tried to excuse her by the fact that the child resembled Lucie, but even when Francis brought the twins over to tea she displayed none of the normal warmth of a grandmother. It was as if she reserved all her affection for her sons, as if her love for them made her incapable of taking anyone else to her heart. Little by little the picture of her with which he had grown up began to blur, as if it had been thrown out of focus, and he was glad when a letter arrived from Sir John Ranken asking him to call and see him on his return to London.

He made this an excuse to leave earlier, and driving back to London was forcibly reminded of the last time he had made an excuse to leave Combe House. Then it had been to see Lucie, now it was to try and forget her.

When the butler ushered him into the drawing-room of Sir John's Hyde Park home, Lady Ranken rose to greet him.

"What a long time since I've seen you, Julian! I hear you did wonders in Washington."

"Not exactly wonders," he smiled. "A combination of persistence and good luck."

"And honest hard work," Sir John put in. A small, spare man with greying hair and a lined face, he looked the Civil Servant he was. "Care for a drink, my boy?"

"Thank you, sir. Whisky, please."

Sir John poured out and they raised glasses to each other.

Conversation was casual until Lady Ranken excused herself. When they were alone Sir John pulled out his pipe and indicated a box of cigarettes to Julian.

"Light up and make yourself comfortable, I want to have a chat with you." He puffed at his pipe, and made sure it was alight. "We were very pleased with the job you did in South America, Julian, it was a difficult piece of negotiation and you came through with flying colours. Washington was a test more than anything else – and you came through that well, too. You've been under me for six years now, Julian. It isn't long as service goes in the Diplomatic Corps – but things are different now – there's a change in outlook. People want action and they want young men to carry it through." He stabbed at Julian with his pipe. "To cut a long story short, Edward Craig is planning to resign and we want you to take over one of the Under-Secretaryships of State."

Julian flushed. "It's a very responsible position, sir. I never expected . . ."

"I need hardly say it's a position that might lead anywhere, depending on how well you fill it. And that brings me to the second point, and one which I confess is less to my liking. What do you intend to do about your marriage?"

Taken by surprise, Julian was at a loss for words. "I don't know – I haven't thought –"

"That's a pity. The best thing would be for you and your

wife to join forces again, but if that's impossible then you should do something about it before you're in the public eye. It'll be fully six months, perhaps a year, before you take up office, and if you're thinking about divorce it would be as well to start procedure right away. Perhaps you can persuade your wife to keep it from the newspapers. The name of Lucie Summerford would mean nothing to the press, but as Lucie Marlow she would attract a good deal of attention." He knocked his pipe into the ashtray. "I haven't liked talking to you this way, Julian. I've always believed a man's private life is private unless it interferes with his work, but in this job I have to see –"

"There's no need to apologise, Sir John," Julian said quickly. "I quite understand. I met my wife in Washington, but unfortunately we couldn't come to an agreement about the future."

"When is she returning to this country?"

"I don't know, but my solicitor can soon find out."

"Good. Otherwise these things have a habit of dragging on for years. You're still a young man, Julian, and you should be married. The right wife is an asset to anyone in your position."

"I wouldn't want to commit myself again in a hurry," Julian said wryly.

"I can appreciate that, and you have my sympathy. Is there definitely no chance of your coming together again?"

"No, sir. There's someone else in her life now."

Sir John stood up. "In that case the quicker the whole thing's finished, the better."

As soon as Julian had gone Lady Ranken came back into the room.

"Well, how did he take it?"

"The new job? He was very pleased."

"And the other?"

Sir John stroked his chin. "It's difficult to tell with Julian – he's so reserved. But it's my impression this marriage of his has gone pretty deep."

"What a pity it failed! She's such a lovely little creature." Lady Ranken bent to fondle the blue Siamese which was rubbing itself against her legs.

"I didn't know you knew her," her husband said in surprise.

"I don't, but when I was waiting for your train the other

day I went to a news-cinema and there were some pictures of her taken in America. It was in connection with some charity or other and several ballerinas allowed themselves to be filmed to help the appeal."

"I can't imagine Julian falling in love with a dancer," Sir John said ruminatively. "He's so quiet and they're such temperamental young women, from what one hears."

Lady Ranken laughed. "She's lovely enough to excuse any temperament!"

"Is she pretty?"

"No, but she's the most ethereal creature I've seen. I don't quite know how to describe it – you have to see her to understand what I mean."

"Ethereal, eh? Hardly the type to stand up to Julian's mother."

His wife sighed. "Even Ann finds her a bit much, and heaven knows she's got plenty of spirit. I'm worried about her, John, I wish there was something I could do."

"Well you can't, so come for a stroll in the garden and stop worrying. If there's one thing the Diplomatic Service has taught me, it's never to interfere in other people's lives unless you have to."

CHAPTER XI

In spite of everything that had gone before, it came as a shock when Lucie received a letter from Charles Blackmer telling her that Julian wanted to divorce her. How final it was, how complete a severance of the ties that had bound them! But there was an even greater cause for the disturbance in that the letter made no mention of Amanda, and she wrote to Blackmer by return, asking him exactly what stand the Summerfords were going to make over the child and pointing out that as she could now provide for Amanda she was determined to fight for her.

It was only when she discussed it with Piers that she realised the case would not be so simple.

"Has it dawned on you, darling, that if Julian divorces you, you may find it difficult to get Amanda?"

"In what way?"

"Only that in the eyes of the law the guilty party can't have custody of the child unless there's some mutual agreement."

"But you know he'd never agree to my having her! And even if I could persuade him, his mother would say no." She stood up and paced the room as he had seen her do so many times. "Oh, why didn't I think of all this sooner! What can I do?"

"Try and stop worrying until you get home. I'm sure Blackmer will think of something." He put his hand under her chin and tilted it up. "Be hopeful, darling. Everything will come all right in the end."

"I hope so, Piers. I couldn't bear it if it didn't."

Lucie went to see Charles Blackmer as soon as she arrived in London.

"Well, well, Mrs. Summerford, you've certainly set the world on fire since I last saw you!" He shook her hand warmly. "Do sit down. I take it you've come to see me about your divorce?"

"Yes." She spoke quickly and nervously, not giving herself time to feel embarrassed. "There's something I want to ask you. Julian will be divorcing me, and I want to know if he can prevent my getting Amanda because of it."

Blackmer pursed his lips. "On the face of it, yes, but it's rather a difficult question to answer *prima facie*. You could appeal, of course, to the court, but whether or not the judge would exercise discretion in your favour I wouldn't like to say."

"Do you think I stand a chance?"

"A great deal depends on the judge you get. Why not let me write to Mr. Summerford's solicitors and tell them you'd like an opportunity to discuss it with your husband?"

"I'd rather not see Julian."

"You might not be able to avoid it. An interview with him, however distasteful, would be preferable to long-drawn litigation splashed all over the front pages of every paper in the country."

"When you put it like that you leave me no choice."

"Is there no chance of your coming together again?"

"No."

"I see. Well, in that case I'll send off a letter today and let you know as soon as I hear." He walked with her to the door. "Good-bye, my dear, and rest assured I'll do all I can."

Sitting in the taxi on her way back to the flat she had taken near Hyde Park, Lucie hoped against hope that Julian would agree to settle Amanda's future amicably.

As she let herself into the flat her maid came out into the hall.

"There are some visitors to see you, Miss Marlow. Shall I bring tea?"

"I'd better see who it is first."

Lucie fixed the pins more securely into the coil at the nape of her neck and opened the drawing-room door. A slim, dark-haired figure rose from the sofa and Lucie flew across the room.

"Ann, how wonderful to see you! You haven't changed a bit!"

Ann kissed her affectionately, then drew back. "You have, though – you're so sophisticiated you make me feel like a country bumpkin!"

"Nonsense, you look lovely."

"Hear, hear!"

Lucie glanced round and saw the man by the window. "Simon! I'm so sorry, I didn't see you."

He smiled and came forward. "I thought I'd better make myself known before you two launched into a spate of gossip."

Lucie laughed. "You're very welcome to join in! Where's Francis and the twins?"

Ann glanced at Simon. "The boys are with my parents and Francis is still in Devon. I've left him." At the startled look on Lucie's face she smiled wryly. "Yes, I know I said I wouldn't part him from the children, but when I found I was beginning to expect the poor little blighters to make up to me for what I was missing, I realised I was in danger of becoming like my mother-in-law. So I packed up, took the twins with me, and left. Anyway, I love Simon too much to have gone on as we were. I've asked Francis for a divorce and in the meantime I'm staying with my parents. I only came to town today because Simon was passing through on his way to Scotland."

"Scotland?"

"Yes. We can't be together yet, so the further apart we are the better. When I've got my divorce we're going out to New Zealand. Simon's uncle has a farm there and he wants someone to run it for him."

"And the boys?"

"They'll go with us, I hope. I don't expect Francis will want to keep them. His mother never liked them, you know."

"Then everything's settled?"

"Not yet, but I hope it soon will be. Francis has gone back to Combe House already. I don't think it'll take him long to get over my departure – poor fool, I still don't think he knows what's hit him, in spite of the fact that it's been brewing under his nose for years." She shrugged. "Now that's enough about my affairs, tell me all about yourself. I've followed your career in the papers, but I want to know about you and Julian. Any developments since I last heard from you?"

Lucie looked down at her hands. "As a matter of fact I've just seen my solicitor. Julian wants a divorce, and I'm hoping we'll come to some arrangement about Amanda." She raised her eyes. "Have you seen her lately?"

"I'm afraid not, darling. You know I never went to Combe House, and that dragon of a nurse would never bring her to see me."

"Have you seen anything of Julian?"

"He came over just before I left Mayfields. I told him a few home truths and he got up and walked out."

Lucie turned away to ring for tea. "Still the same old Julian. I don't suppose he'll ever change. Well, there's nothing I can do about it, and the sooner I realise it the happier I'll be." Then with a sudden change of tone: "Ah, here's Ellen with the tea. I hope Simon comes back before it gets cold."

With her whole heart Lucie was glad for Ann. But she would not have been human if she had not envied the way her sister-in-law's problems were being resolved. If only hers could be settled as easily!

From Charles Blackmer she heard nothing and although longing to see Amanda, she knew it would be foolish to go down to Combe House until he had arranged for her to do so. The large, beautifully dressed doll she had bought in New York was still in its cellophane wrapping and every day she looked at it and wondered how long it would be before she could give it to her baby.

CHAPTER XII

WITHIN a fortnight of their return to England the company was back at work. Seats for the opening night were sold out weeks in advance and Lucie found that fame had its proverbial penalties, for she could scarcely call her soul her own.

It was several weeks before Charles Blackmer wrote and told her that Julian had agreed to meet her, and he'd suggested she come down to Combe House and see Amanda at the same time. Surely that meant he was willing for her to have some part in the child's future? If not, there could be no point in asking her to go down.

As she was appearing in *Swan Lake*, she arranged to go down to Devon the following weekend and spent the rest of the week in such a ferment of anxiety that she had to unburden herself to Piers.

He was furious when he heard.

"Must you go to that house again?"

"I have no choice. The only way I can get Amanda is to try and make Julian settle out of court."

"If you're hoping to convince him you'll bring up the child better than his mother, you're crazy!"

She pushed back her hair. "I don't want to go, Piers, but Charles Blackmer thinks I ought to, and the sooner it's over the better."

When Lucie boarded the train at Paddington on Sunday morning she was tense with apprehension. What would Mrs. Summerford think of her now? Lucinda Marlow in her St. Laurent dress and mink coat bore no resemblance to the nonentity who had run away over two years ago. Yet she was just as nervous as she had been that first day when Julian had taken her home, and as she stepped into the taxi at Teincombe station she would willingly have turned tail and fled had it not been for Amanda.

Her hands were moist as she paid off the driver and rang the bell, but to Julian, as she stepped through the front door, she looked infinitely more poised and lovely than he had ever known her. It was the first time he had seen her in furs, and the soft skins against her face gave it a pearly radiance.

"Hullo, Julian." Lucie held out her hand. "Sorry I'm late, but the train was slow. The usual Sunday service."

"I thought you might come by road."

"No, it would have taken too long, and driving is so tiring." Although her manner was matter-of-fact she was quick to notice the network of lines around his eyes and a touch of grey in his hair which had not been there when they had met a few short months ago. "You're looking tired, Julian."

He led her into the drawing-room. "I've been working hard."

"No holiday after your American trip?"

"A brief one, but I'm at it again now. I've been – I'm being appointed Under-Secretary of State."

"Congratulations! I must have missed it in the papers."

"It hasn't been made public yet. That's one of the reasons I wanted to see you."

He moved nervously around the room as he spoke. It was strange to see Lucie here again, her small feet sedately crossed, her fair head with its absurd little green hat resting against the tapestry cover of the sofa.

Her voice broke in on his thoughts. "May I go up and see Amanda, please?"

"Of course. We'll go up now, before tea."

Apart from Nurse Richards, who withdrew in silence as soon as they entered, there was no one in the nursery except Amanda. And what a different, adorable Amanda! Lucie swept the child up in her arms, heedless of her weight, heedless of the lovely coat or the hat which the little fingers seized and immediately threw to the floor.

"Darling Amanda! Do you remember me? It's Mummy come to see you!"

The grey eyes so like her own regarded her solemnly. "Seen lady in picture books."

It was the first time Lucie had heard Amanda speak, and at the sound of the clear, light voice her throat contracted. "What does she mean?"

"The newspapers," Julian explained. "I've shown her some of your photographs."

Lucie sat down with the child on her knee. "My, you're a big girl now – I can't hold you for very long."

"I'se nearly free."

"I know you are, my darling." She reached behind for the doll she had brought. "Look what I have for you. Do you like it?"

For the first time the little girl showed some excitement. "It's pretty! Is it mine?"

"Your very own."

Feverishly the small hands tore away the wrappings and the fair head bent intently over the doll's vacant pink features and stiff body. "Her dress is like mine – look, Daddy, it's like mine!"

"She has a petticoat too." Lucie stood up and threw her coat over a chair, then sat on the floor and Amanda scrambled down at her side.

"Show me the petticoat, Mummy. Is it like mine too?"

"I expect so, darling."

For nearly an hour Lucie sat with her daughter, scarcely aware when Julian left the room. It was not until Nurse Richards reappeared carrying a tray that she realised how long she had been there and got to her feet.

"I'll come up again later, when Amanda's had her tea."

Julian was waiting for her in the drawing-room, and he took her coat and put it over the back of the sofa. "Mink," he said briefly. "Now I can really believe you're a celebrity."

"Did you find it so hard to believe before?"

"Sometimes. Don't forget I only remember you in the corps de ballet, when the first time you danced the Blue Bird was a great event in your life."

"You have a good memory."

"That's not always a good thing."

At that moment Gladys wheeled in the tea-trolley and Julian nodded to Lucie.

"Will you pour out?"

She hesitated. "If you want me to."

It was a long time since she had poured tea for Julian, and her hand shook imperceptibly as she picked up the milk jug. She had passed him his cup when the door opened and her mother-in-law came in, the tall figure with its bland, handsome face exactly as she had remembered.

"How do you do, Lucie?" Mrs. Summerford's voice was cool. "Don't bother to pour out the tea now I'm here."

"I thought you weren't coming, Mother," Julian said awkwardly.

"I'm no later than usual, dear."

"No milk for me, please," Lucie put in quickly.

"Of course, you must be careful of your figure."

"Naturally. It's my livelihood."

The bird-like glance took in the expensive dress and the fur coat draped across the sofa. "It certainly seems lucrative. I can understand why you left us."

"You'll never understand that, Mrs. Summerford."

The woman flushed. "Time hasn't improved your manners, Lucie."

Lucie's retort was forestalled by Francis coming in.

"Good heavens, it's Lucie! You're looking very well."

"Thank you, Francis, so are you." And indeed he was, his open face tanned and smiling, his manner as hearty as she had always remembered it.

Mrs. Summerford pursed her lips. "Francis's looks don't pity him, but he's been through a terrible time. Ann behaved disgracefully. She ran away with Simon Hardy."

"I know," Lucie said flatly. "They've been to see me."

"Indeed? I suppose they came to you for condonement?"

"Not at all. They don't feel they need it."

"Then they're shameless. In my day a woman didn't break up her home and run away with a lover unless –"

"Ann and Simon aren't lovers," Lucie said spiritedly, "and as for Francis going through such a bad time, he saw so little of Ann while she was here that I shouldn't think he notices her absence."

"It wasn't my fault that Francis preferred being with me. You can't blame a man for preferring a harmonious atmosphere to sitting with a nagging wife."

Lucie clenched her hands. "Ann nagged Francis because she was ambitious for him, you left him alone because you wanted to keep him here. No one in their right mind can blame her for running away – you made her life unbearable."

"You were always extreme in your language, Lucie, so I won't bother to argue. I would merely point out that Ann had a home of her own and –"

"You can't have a home without a husband," Lucie said

fiercely, "and you did your best to see she didn't have one!"

Mrs. Summerford put down her cup sharply. "I won't have you talk to me like that! How dare you come into my house and say such things, you wretched girl!"

"It's about time someone told you a few home-truths." All the hurt and humiliation of her own marriage flared up in Lucie. "Your sons might be afraid of hurting your feelings, but I'm not! You can't harm me any more than you've done already. Ann's a fine woman and Francis was lucky to have married her at all. I'm only surprised she stuck it as long as she did."

"And I'm not surprised you defend her. You're both tarred with the same brush – treacherous, faithless women!"

"That's enough, Mother!" Francis's voice rang out so sharply that the two women looked at him in surprise. "I'm not going to sit here and listen to you slandering Ann. She was never faithless, and as for leaving me, heaven knows we gave her enough provocation."

"*We* gave her provocation?"

"Yes, we," he said doggedly. "You know as well as I do that you're as much to blame for my marriage going on the rocks as I am! Lucie's right in everything she says. I let Ann down from the moment I married her because I always put you first. She thought she was marrying a man with a career and an independent position and all she got was a weakling who relied on his mother!"

Mrs. Summerford began to cry. "I never thought I'd hear a son of mine talk to me like that! If Lucie hadn't come here with her venomous lies . . ."

"They're not lies, Mother." Francis spoke more quietly this time. "Lucie's right – I deserved to have lost Ann, and I only hope she's happier with Simon than she was with me."

"That's the most immoral thing I've ever heard!"

"Morality goes deeper than convention, Mother, and it's time you broadened your outlook." He ran a hand over his eyes. "I'd better go before I say something I'll regret."

He flung out of the room and Mrs. Summerford collapsed in sobs.

Lucie stood up and put on her coat. "I'd better go too, Julian. I won't go upstairs and see Amanda again, it'd only mean another parting. Perhaps we can meet in London next week and discuss her future?"

"Very well. I'll run you to the station."

Sitting beside him in the car Lucie felt like weeping. Quarrelling with his mother was the quickest way to antagonise Julian, and by losing her temper she had probably lost Amanda as well. Mrs. Summerford had always been her enemy and after today would have no need to conceal it. Her only consolation was the way Francis had sprung to her defence. What a pity his *volte-face* had come too late! But even the satisfaction of having witnessed it did not alter the fact that her visit had achieved nothing, and she felt she must say something to try and save the situation.

"I'm sorry I argued with your mother, Julian, but everything I said seemed to come out of its own accord."

"There's no need to apologise." He steered the car into the station yard and opened the door for her. "I'll be in touch with you, Lucie."

"Very well." She held out her hand, withdrawing it almost as their fingers met. "Good-bye, Julian."

To Lucie's surprise Piers was waiting for her at Paddington.

"I thought you might be in need of a little moral support."

"I could do with cheering up," she admitted.

"As bad as that?"

"Wait till I tell you!"

Over a table at a small French restaurant in Soho, she recounted the events of the day.

"I know I shouldn't have lost my temper," she concluded, "but I defended Ann instinctively! In a way I was defending myself too."

"You couldn't have chosen a worse time! Summerford will never give in now."

"Then I'll fight him." Her mouth set. "You haven't any children, Piers, so you can't understand – but I'll stop at nothing to get Amanda back."

"I understand very well – perhaps better than you think."

As soon as they had finished their meal they drove back to Lucie's flat and Piers sat down on the sofa while Lucie took up her usual position on a cushion by the fire. Conversation was spasmodic, each busy with their own thoughts, and after about half an hour he stood up to go.

In the hall she leant against him, her voice muffled in his jacket.

"Thank you for being my Father Confessor, Piers, I don't know what I'd do without you."

"You'll never have to do without me. I'm here as long as you need me." He pulled her into his arms. "You can't go on regretting the past, Lucie. You're too great a dancer to lock your emotions in an Ivory Tower. I love you and need you, and I'm conceited enough to think that you need me."

"I do, Piers, I do. I can't live the rest of my life like this, and there's no one else I'd rather share it with. I don't love you as I loved Julian, but if you still want to marry me when I'm free. . . ."

"There's no 'if' about it, my darling," he spoke the words against her mouth, "I'll take you on any terms."

His kiss was long and deep, but Lucie could not surrender to his mood, and as if conscious of her failure to do so, he drew away.

"You're tired, dearest. Go to bed and try to forget everything. I'll see you in the morning."

His footsteps died away and Lucie went back into the drawing-room. How lonely the flat was! Not even the lovely furnishings and exquisite flowers could make it into a home. The fat silk cushions, and tall hangings at the windows looked back at her vacantly. Would her marriage to Piers bring her the happiness she had lost? She only knew it would be preferable to this emptiness, and with a sigh she switched off the lights and went into her room.

Driving back to Combe House, Julian's mind was full of the afternoon's events. In spite of having asked his mother not to cause any unpleasantness during Lucie's visit, she had purposely set out to rile the girl, and he was furiously angry. So angry that he had felt no surprise when easy-going, good-natured Francis had rounded on her in defence of Ann. Well, it was time he faced facts too. For the past few months he had been groping in a maze of complexities and obligations. Today had served to set him free.

He parked his car in the garage and walked into the house

to find his mother still huddled on the settee. Her tears had given way to tight-lipped annoyance and she looked up unsmilingly as he came in.

"Did you *have* to drive that woman to the station?"

"I don't *have* to do anything."

"Be careful how you talk to me, Julian! I've had quite enough for one day."

"If you don't mind my saying so, you brought it on yourself."

"That's a cruel thing to say!"

"It was cruel of you to talk about Ann like that in front of Francis."

"Rubbish! Any normal man would have agreed with me. I wasn't to know that my own son would defend a wife who had deserted him."

He sat down. "Francis is probably just beginning to realise that Ann *had* good reason for leaving him, and I'm inclined to agree."

"Agree!" It was an outraged cry. "I suppose you'll agree that Lucie was right when she ran away and left you with a helpless baby?"

"She didn't leave the helpless baby, Mother, we took Amanda away from her."

"And I suppose that was wrong too?"

"No," he conceded, "we were right there. But I was wrong in not waiting to see Lucie first."

"When she came back from her lover?"

He flinched. "Piers isn't her lover."

"So she'd like you to believe! Oh, Julian, don't blame yourself. Don't imagine something in Lucie that was never there! When you married her you were infatuated, but surely you can see now that she's no wife for a man like you?"

"On the contrary, she'd be a great asset to me. But I didn't marry to help my career. I married for love."

"What does a woman like that know of love? If you love someone you want to do things for them. You make sacrifices, like I have –"

"And then use them as your weapons!"

Her breath caught in her throat. "I never thought I'd live to see both my sons turn on me like this! You can't say much horrible things, Julian – you've got to see it from my point of view."

"All I've ever done is see it from your point of view! Now I think it's time I saw it from mine – and Lucie's and Ann's and Francis's!"

His voice rose and she stared at him in fear. "Julian, stop shouting, calm yourself!"

"How can you expect me to be calm when I see the mess I've made of my life – when I know I've lost everything through my own blind stupidity? I wish to God I'd never brought Lucie down here!"

"Is that all the thanks I get for everything I've done for you?"

"Do you want me to thank you for breaking up my marriage?"

For a moment Mrs. Summerford could not speak. Then with an effort she controlled herself. "I don't know what you're talking about, Julian. How could I have broken up your marriage? From the moment Lucie came here I knew it would fail, if it hadn't been for me she'd have run away sooner. You always said I was tactful, but you don't know half of what I had to put up with. I hid everything from you because I wanted to spare you. Even when she tried to get rid of the baby –"

"*Be quiet,* Mother," he shouted, "you've said enough! That's a monstrous lie. She never did anything of the kind!"

"You agreed with me once."

"Because I was mad!" He passed a hand over his eyes. "God, when I remember the things I said to her, I'm surprised she's ever spoken to me again."

"Would you be so concerned if she didn't?"

"I'd regret it all my life."

"What does that mean?"

"That I'm going to do everything I can to get her back!"

With startling suddenness she rounded on him. "If you go to that woman, Julian, I wash my hands of you! You can take your child and never come back."

"You don't mean that, Mother! You're overwrought."

He took a step towards her, but she warded him off. "I *do* mean it, Julian – you must choose between Lucie and me. If you want her so much you'll have to manage without me for the rest of your life."

"Is that your last word?"

"Yes."

He turned towards the door.

"Julian!" she cried. "Where are you going?"

"To Lucie."

"Can you leave me as easily as that?"

"Not easily, Mother, but you give me no alternative."

Her face swelled with rage. "Go to her, then, go, go, go! Make your life with a worthless slut who deserted you and tried to kill your unborn child! Go to the creature who's robbed you of your self-respect! I wish you well of her! You've thrown away all my years of sacrifice and given me nothing in return! Cast me off in my old age, I don't care! You're not worthy of me! I don't want you any longer!" She threw herself on the sofa in a paroxysm of rage and beat her hands against the cushions.

Julian moved over and knelt at her side. "Mother, don't cry. It won't make any difference to my decision. It's taken me a long time to learn that a man can love two women without being disloyal to either one. You're my mother and I love you as man should love the woman who's brought him into the world. But Lucie's my wife and my future is with her and Amanda. I'm going to ask her to come back to me. If she refuses I shan't harbour any bitterness against you because I've been as much to blame, but whatever happens I'll go on loving her, and nothing you can say or do will alter that."

Still his mother said nothing, and he went on: "I'll be leaving very early in the morning and taking Amanda with me. If Lucie does come back to me don't ever expect me to bring her here. The only way our marriage will have a chance is for her to forget everything that's happened in the past. But I'll be back one day, Mother – not from a sense of duty but because whatever you've done you're still part of my life and my love for Lucie will never change it. If you remember that, you won't be jealous of her any more."

He stood up, touched his lips to the lowered head and left.

Promptly at eight o'clock next morning he drove away from Combe House with Amanda and Nurse Richards in the back of the car. At the top of the hill he turned to take a last look at his old home. One day he would come back; his realisation of his mother's treachery was too recent for him to conciliate her yet.

Every mile that brought him nearer to Lucie increased his longing to see her. His awakening had been slow, but now it had come it was all the more complete. She had accused him of being immature and how right she had been! What hope had he of regaining her love and convincing her that his change of heart was true – how could he make her believe he was no longer blinded by his obsession for his mother?

Arriving in London, he installed Amanda and the nurse in a hotel before going to the theatre to book a seat for the performance.

The girl in the box office looked at him in surprise. "Gracious, sir, not one left!"

Such a contingency had never crossed his mind. "Do you mean you're completely sold out?"

"Have been for weeks."

"What about returns?"

"Not a chance. It's as difficult to get in for Lucie Marlow as a Cup Final."

With a brief smile Julian walked out of the foyer. Lucie would get him in if he asked her, but he could not do so without explaining why he had come and it would be disastrous to upset her before a performance. Yet he passionately wanted to see her dance.

Suddenly he thought of Bellamy. Should he swallow his pride and send the man a note, or wait miserably in his car until the ballet was over? The prospect was so dismal that he hunted in his pocket for a card, scribbled something on the back and handed it in at the stage door.

Almost immediately the doorkeeper beckoned him in. "Mr. Bellamy'll see you right away. Down the corridor, up the three steps at the end, second door on the right."

Julian walked past him into the labyrinth of corridors, found the room without difficulty, and after a moment's hesitation knocked on the door.

"Come in!"

He obeyed, and found himself in a small, bright-lit room with two easy chairs and a large dressing-table running along one side of the wall.

Piers was putting the finishing touches to his make-up and regarded him through the mirror. "Unexpected social call, Summerford?"

"I've come to ask a favour."

"I don't guarantee to oblige, but ask away."

"I want a seat tonight. I've tried every possible means of getting one, but the ticket agencies are closed and the box office is sold out."

"Does Lucie know you're here?"

"No. I didn't want to upset her before the performance."

"Commendable consideration." The dancer straddled his chair and faced him. "I don't want to appear presumptuous, but why are you suddenly so interested in seeing Lucie dance? Or are you such a keen balletomane that you couldn't bear to miss her *Giselle*?"

"I don't give a damn what the ballet is! If you must know I've come to talk to her tonight and I'd like to see her dance first."

"Won't another night do?"

"Damn it, no! If Lucie doesn't – can't give me the answer I want, I won't ever see her again." He stood up. "However, if it's too much to ask . . ."

Piers reached for a cigarette and lit it. He had only to say that Lucie had promised to marry him for Summerford to get up and disappear out of both their lives. But could he have it on his conscience to part her from the only man she had ever really loved? And what of the child – would it be right to rob Amanda of either of her parents?

With sudden decision he stubbed out his cigarette. "There's a couple of things I'd like to tell you, Summerford. When Lucie came back yesterday she agreed to marry me – no, wait a minute, let me finish. I'm well aware that she only did so because she couldn't see any future with you, especially after what had happened at Combe House." He lit another cigarette. "One other point I'd like to clear up. Lucie and I have never been lovers. She needed someone to lean on and I was there at the right time. That was all."

"And that was enough for you?"

"I hoped she'd grow to love me. It wasn't until you'd met in Washington that I knew there was no hope. Lucie and I have never been more than friends."

"Thank you for telling me."

"I'm doing it for Lucie, not for you." Piers turned back to the mirror. "I suppose you realise she won't give up her work quite as willingly as she did the first time?"

"I wouldn't expect her to. She's too fine an artist."

"And would you mind if she continued to dance with me?"

"Not if you don't."

A gleam of unwilling admiration came into Piers' eyes. "That's something I shall have to decide for myself, but thanks for the compliment. As a matter of fact, I've had an offer to make a film in Hollywood and it only needed something like this to make me accept it. Frankly, I doubt if I could work with Lucie if she goes back to you. If she doesn't, that's another story." He went to the door and shouted for the call-boy. "Johnny! Take this gentleman to one of the V.I.P. seats." He turned to Julian. "Good-bye, Summerford, and I hope you enjoy the performance."

"Good-bye, Bellamy. I can never thank you enough."

"Just make Lucie happy."

Julian got to his seat as the curtain went up, and from the moment Lucie appeared on the stage he was conscious of no one else.

As a village girl in love with a young rustic she was the epitome of grace and innocence, charmingly questioning the marguerites – he loves me, he loves me not – as the white petals fluttered down. Discovering her beloved to be a nobleman who could never marry her, she killed herself with his sword and died as the first act came to a close.

The curtain rose again to reveal the banks of a pool silvered by moonlight, and as midnight chimed Giselle threw off her shroud and joined with the Wilis in their nocturnal dance. A haunting refrain announced the appearance of her lover and the spirits began to entice him into the lake. Frantically Giselle signed him to embrace the cross upon her grave, but forced by the Queen of the Wilis to lure him from his sanctuary, she danced with such grace and seduction that he left the cross and went towards her. There followed a pas de deux of passionate abandon, a frenzy of hopeless love which ended as the pale streaks of dawn drew the spirits away and the lover escaped, leaving Giselle covered by the flowers on her grave.

Julian had seen *Giselle* many times before but never had he been so moved. Lucie had danced with a tragic intensity that placed her in the front rank of her profession; not a single conventional gesture, not one false movement. Incredible that he had ever held that frail body in his arms and aroused it with his desire, difficult to understand his own folly in repudiating her.

Jerked back to his surroundings by the deafening applause, he cheered with the rest of the audience as the curtain rose again and again. That is my wife, my darling, he thought, and his pride in her was mingled with bitter self-reproach.

At last the clapping died away and he edged through the crowded gangway into the street. A large crowd was gathered outside the stage door, but the doorman recognised him and nodded as he shouldered his way past and walked down the corridor to the principal dressing-room.

Lucie's dresser opened the door and before she knew what was happening found herself in the corridor with a pound note in her hand. Julian turned the key in the lock, leant back against the door and looked at Lucie.

Unfamiliar in the diaphanous costume, she was untying the laces of her ballet shoes as she turned and saw him.

In her exotic make-up, the eyebrows and hazel eyes heavily shaded like a doll's, she was a stranger, and Julian felt the impetus of his courage ebbing away.

"Lucie, I want to talk to you – I –"

There was a loud knocking at the door and without a word she went across and unlocked it to admit the dresser with an armful of flowers.

"Sorry, sir, but I had to come back. Room'll look like a florist's if we don't get rid of some of these." She dumped the bouquets on the floor. "No room in the wash-basin. Will you be taking any of them home with you tonight, Miss Marlow?"

"Just the roses, Judy. You can send the rest to the hospital as usual." She turned to Julian. "We can talk about Amanda when I've changed. Will you wait outside – I'll meet you at the stage door."

Feeling he had bungled everything Julian waited in the corridor. Could Bellamy have been wrong – did Lucie's cool reception mean she was indifferent to him after all? Yet remembering what had happened when they had last met, he should have been surprised that she was even civil.

He had begun to think she had forgotten he was there when she finally appeared, her mink coat around her shoulders, her face pale without the heavy make-up. But even then they were not free to go, for at the stage door she was surrounded by a struggling mob of fans who clamoured for her autograph and it was only when he had drawn his car up at the kerb that she managed to extricate herself with smiling excuses.

As they drove off she leant back with a sigh.

"Tired?" he asked.

"*Giselle*'s rather strenuous."

"You were wonderful, Lucie."

"Thank you."

Nothing more was said until he drew up at the entrance to the block of flats where she lived, and he followed her in silence across the lobby and up in the lift.

She opened the door of her flat and led him through the hall into the large, pale-coloured lounge. A standard lamp shed a pool of light over the pastel furnishings and white fur rug in front of the fireplace, and he could not help contrasting this elegance with the shabby dilapidation of the boarding-house where she had been living when he had first met her. Seeing her in this gracious setting brought home to him how far she had come since he had married her. What a fool he was to hope she would want him again when she could have any man she set her heart on!

Lucie slipped off her coat and indicated the cocktail cabinet. "Have a drink?"

He shook his head. "But don't let me stop you."

"I must have something to eat first." She sank on to the sofa. "Do sit down."

"I'd rather stand if you don't mind."

There was an uncomfortable pause. "If you've come to talk about Amanda, let's get it over." She pushed back a strand of hair with a familiar gesture and all at once she was Lucie again, not the ballerina with whom he was so ill at ease. "Are you going to let me have her part of the year, Julian?"

He walked unsteadily to the window. "You can have Amanda for ever if you'll take me as well!"

He did not dare turn and look at her, and her voice when she spoke seemed to come from a long way off.

"I'm going to marry Piers."

He faced her. "I know. I saw him tonight before the performance, and he told me everything."

"Everything?" A sudden thought struck her and she got up and reached for her handbag. "I almost forgot – Judy gave me a note from him."

He watched as she took out an envelope and extracted the single sheet of notepaper, raising her eyes slowly to his when she had read it. "You'd no right to go and see him, Julian, no right at all."

"I didn't go with the intention of talking about you, I just wanted to ask him for a seat." He ran a hand nervously across his face. "I had to see the performance tonight, Lucie. I don't know why, but I had to see you dance before I asked you to come back to me."

"I'm afraid it's too late."

"You don't mean that! For God's sake, Lucie, you can't mean it!" He went towards her, but she backed away.

"I do mean it. It's quite impossible for us to start again – I'm not the same person any more."

"Neither am I," he said eagerly. "I've left Combe House for good. You must have wondered why I never said a word when I dropped you at the station on Sunday, but it wasn't because I disagreed with you, my darling, it was because I was too confused to talk to you properly. I couldn't believe that Francis had woken up to the truth before me. I've no excuse for not having seen that Mother was to blame for our marriage going on the rocks – I've been a damn fool, Lucie, but I've woken up now!" The words poured out. "You're the only one who means anything to me and I can't live my life without you. I'm not asking you to give up your career. I only want you to take me back and give me another chance. You can live where you like and do what you like if only you'll take me back!"

"But your job –"

"I won't be posted abroad in my new position. We can live in London and you can go on working. I've brought Amanda with me – she's waiting for you, darling, and so am I." Quite suddenly the flood of words stopped and he sat down and buried his head in his hands. "Forgive me, Lucie, I don't know what I'm saying. I've no right to come here and talk to you like this after the way I've treated you."

His voice was dull and lifeless, and Lucie could not believe that this defeated, unhappy man was the Julian she remembered, the Julian who had always been so reserved and controlled.

"When I remember the things I said in Washington I'm surprised you can even bring yourself to see me." His words were muffled in his hands. "I've said and done every rotten thing a man can say and do to a woman and I've only myself to blame that you left me. The only foolish thing you ever did was to marry me. I'm no good to you, Lucie, and I know it! I should never have come here in the first place."

He stood up and moved blindly to the door, but with a rustle of skirts she barred his way.

"Julian, listen to me. A woman doesn't always marry the man who's right for her. It's got nothing to do with ambition or success or even sharing the same things; it's part of a longing that only one man can satisfy. I've hated you and despised you but never forgotten you, although God knows I've tried. You've been obsessed with your mother and now you want me to believe that you're not. Well, I don't think I can. I still think there'll be times when you'll compare us, when you'll wish you could run away and become a little boy again. I don't believe you're a man yet, Julian, but if you want to be – if you're willing to fight then I'll come back and help you." With a convulsive exclamation she gave him her hands. "Oh, God, Julian, I love you, and there's nothing I can do about it!"

Then they were in each other's arms, her cheeks wet against his. For a long time they remained close, two strangers bound by the single memory of their desire. Later there would be explanations, promises. At the moment they were together with the future before them, and Piers and Mrs. Summerford fast receding shadows.

It was three years since they had kissed, three years of heartache and unfulfilled desire, and no touching of hands and lips could assuage their longing.

He drew away shakily. "I can't believe we're here, like this. That you should still want me . . . a fool . . . a boy when you are so much a woman . . . oh, Lucie, what an idiot I've been!"

"Not an idiot, darling, just blind and obstinately loyal."

"That loyalty belongs to you now. Everything I am and ever will be belongs to you." He kissed her fingers. "I don't want to start dictating to you, my dearest, but I want to take you away – be alone with you – the two of us together."

Her mouth trembled into a smile. "This is one time I won't refuse you. Even if Dennison says no, I'll still come!"

"I'm so proud of you, Lucie. When I watched you dance tonight I wanted to tell the world you were my wife." His eyes twinkled. "You'd better make the most of your success while you can though, because you'll soon be having a rival. I think Amanda's going to follow in your footsteps!"

"When we have a son he'll follow in yours!" She drew his head down, her face suffused with tenderness, as if the very bones were melting with love. "Let's go to Paris, Julian. We were happiest there and I never thought I'd see it again with you."

"When we come back this time it'll be to Amanda and a home of our own."

All the problems dissolved in the magic of the last phrase.